THE HUNTER

MONSTERS AND BEAUTIES

JENIKA SNOW

THE HUNTER (Monsters and Beauties)

By Jenika Snow

www.JenikaSnow.com

Jenika_Snow@Yahoo.com

Copyright © September 2022 by Jenika Snow

First E-book and Paperback Publication: September 2022

Cover Designer: Haya in Designs

Editors: Snow Queen Editing

Beta Readers: Judy Ann Loves Books

Proof Reader: Jill Reading, All Encompassing Books

What if the big bad wolf kidnapped Little Red Riding Hood solely for his pleasure?

After my grandmother passed away, it left me with this feeling of emptiness. I had a dead-end job, no friends or family, and I was trying to navigate this new world while being utterly alone.

The perfect solution? Take a once in a lifetime trip to Alaska and reconnect with the wilderness and all the things that make me happy.

Being isolated in a cabin with no electricity, running water, or cell service sounded perfect until I roughed it in the wild and realized this might not have been the best idea.

Things were going great until they weren't, and I realized I wasn't alone. It was the hunter, and I was its prey.

And when I finally came face-to face with my

stalker, it wasn't anything I could have pictured in my wildest dreams.

He was a monster, a literal furry, huge werewolf looking beast that said he chose me as his mate, and I was now his.

It took me to his lair where he touched me, licked me... gave me pleasure. And despite knowing I had to fight him and this new reality, I wanted more.

Wolf might be terrifying to look at, bigger and stronger than anything I could ever imagine, but his sole purpose was to please me.

The real question was, did I ever want to go back to civilization and the life I once knew?

* A Little Red Riding Hood Reimagining.

PROLOGUE

Marcella

I stumbled back, tripping over my own feet as the creature came closer. I fell on my ass but didn't stop retreating, my lungs burning as I hyperventilated.

The creature was wolf-like, but... not. It was some monstrous animal/human hybrid that was plucked out of my damn nightmares.

It came closer, his body hunched over as it walked on all fours.

When the thick trunk of a tree stopped me from retreating, I wanted to scream, to fight back. But I was terrified, unable to move, this cold dread washing over me.

When it was ten feet from me it stopped, the shadows of nightfall shrouding too much of this beast. I could make out its massive body and inhuman head, and see a longer face, snout, sharp teeth, and fur covering its entire form.

And then the thing slowly rose to stand on two hind legs, its calves angled like wolves' so they looked bent.

It came closer; the ground vibrating from how powerful its steps were. The thing had to be at least seven feet tall, with bulging arms, and hands that were more like paws tipped with black claws. It had a thick, furry tail that was moving back and forth, reminiscent of a predator about to pounce.

God... the thing was *naked* and aroused, and what hung between its legs was massive.

"No," I whispered and shook my head, holding my hands out as if that would actually ward it off.

I trailed my gaze up its barreled chest and to its wolf-like face.

Holy shit.

Although it looked like a wolf—*werewolf,* my mind whispered—it held very clear intelligence behind its dark eyes as it watched me.

"Oh God. Please. Please don't hurt me." My voice was whisper-thin. I wasn't even sure I'd spoken the words aloud. "W-what are you?" It was so close now that all I smelled was this wild scent that clung to it.

Here was this primitive creature crowding me, breathing on me... refusing to give me space. It was going to eat me. I was sure of it. Why else would it be here? What other purpose would it have for me?

Not it. *He*. This creature was clearly male given what he was working with.

"I'm the one who is going to make you mine."

I shook my head and lashed out, raking my nails along his chest, feeling hard, defined muscle underneath. He was fast as he snapped his paw out and curled it around my wrist, my palm and fingers so tiny compared to his.

I felt this survival instinct rise as I started to scream and kick out, but I was like an annoying gnat compared to him, I was sure.

And when he let go of my wrist to grab my ankle, stopping my foot from connecting with the huge thing he had between his legs, I screamed again. But this time it was in fear. Bone-chilling fear.

He stood and started dragging me away like I was a damn sack of potatoes.

I twisted my body, clawing at the ground, dirt digging underneath my nails. Tears made my vision blurry, and then the world turned as he lifted me up and threw me over his shoulder.

For a second, the wind was knocked out of me as my stomach connected with his shoulder, and I lay there flopping around from his movements.

And then he picked up speed, running, so it forced me to grip the long, dark fur that covered him and hold on, sobbing uncontrollably.

"Don't worry, female. I'll have you crying for a far different reason soon enough."

CHAPTER
ONE

Marcella

T thought I'd gotten used to death.

The initial pain. That horrible ache in the center of your chest that just didn't seem to ease no matter how much time passed.

But as I watched them lower my grandmother's casket into the ground... it hurt.

I stayed at the cemetery long after everyone had left, sitting on the ground with my knees pulled up to my chest and my arms wrapped around my legs.

I'd been close with my grandmother. She raised me when my mother hadn't been fit to do the job.

Blanchette had shown me how to ride a bike, and even helped me buy my first tampons when I got my period and explained it all to me when I started crying because I didn't know what was happening.

She sat down and talked with me about boys, showed me how to drive, and helped me with my homework every single night. And when I graduated from high school, she was the only family I had there, but she's the only one I'd wanted.

For all intents and purposes, she was my mother.

And now, at twenty-two, I was utterly and truly alone.

I wiped an errant tear that slipped down my cheek and felt my heart continuously break, the shearing pain of it ripping into a million unique pieces.

They always said with time it got easier, but right now I couldn't even imagine it ever being better. I literally had no one else. I hadn't seen my mother since she dropped me off at my grandmother's when I was just a child.

My father hadn't been in the picture and had been an only child. Hell, I wouldn't even call my "friends" more than acquaintances, only seeing them at work.

I stood and brushed the grass and dirt off my

bottom, glancing down at my legs to see a run in my dark stockings.

I guess it was par for the course on how things were going for me.

My secondhand black Mary Jane shoes had scuff marks, and my dress, one I bought at the thrift store yesterday, had a stain on the side and the hem was fraying at the bottom.

"Well," I said to myself, since I was alone, staring at the mound of dirt before me, "I'm going to keep thinking about all the things you said. And remember that boys can suck at any age, and that just because the sun sets and everything gets dark, it'll still rise the next day and brighten everything up again."

Brushing another tear away, I smiled.

"And I'm always gonna remember how you taught me how to make your famous chocolate chip cookies, even though I burn them every single time."

I smoothed my hands down my dress and took in a deep breath, then exhaled slowly.

"But let's be real. I'll never get it right. Not like how you always did." I laughed softly as I pictured my grandmother standing in front of me, scolding me for bringing myself down. Her face would get even more wrinkled as she told me never to be negative toward myself, that there's always room for improvement and that's how we grow... by trying repeatedly.

I turned and left without another backward glance, because I knew if I did, I wouldn't stop myself from really breaking down.

A new chapter of my life started now, and I'd try to make the most of it. But truthfully?

It really fucking sucked.

CHAPTER
TWO

Marcella

"Aren't you scared to do that by yourself?"

One of my coworkers looked over my shoulder at my phone.

I pulled up a map of the area in Ketchikan, Alaska, where I'd be staying.

When I'd found out my grandma had left me a small, but comfortable, inheritance, I knew taking a trip was what she'd want me to do. It wasn't much, but it included her two-bedroom house, the small piece of land the home sat on, and a few thousand dollars.

I'd cried when the lawyer told me, not because it was too much or too little, but because even after

9

she'd passed away, she was still wanting to take care of me.

She'd been pinching pennies for a long time since she was on a fixed income, so knowing she'd been putting money into an account for me had me breaking down right in the attorney's office.

So this trip was just as much for me as it was in memory of her.

"Why would I be scared? Over eight hundred thousand tourists a year, just from the cruise ships alone, see Ketchikan. They even have cruise ships that stop."

I didn't bother mentioning the fact the cabin I rented was actually on an island. I'd have to take a boat there, which would be a half-hour trip, and there wouldn't be any civilization for miles. Not to mention no electricity or cell service.

No, Tara didn't need to know any of that, because she was already staring at me like I had lost my mind wanting to go to Alaska.

Hell, she was probably one of those people who thought it was nothing but tundra and that you had to wear head to toe thermal gear or you'd freeze to death.

"The places I'm staying at have tourists." I

shrugged. "Besides, I used to do a lot of hikes and go camping with my grandmother."

Tara's brows lifted as she tried—and failed—not to drag her gaze up and down my body.

I held in my snort of indignation and instead narrowed my eyes because I knew exactly what she was thinking.

"You're a big girl. How did you *do any hiking?"*

I waited, silently hoping she'd say something along those lines because I'd make sure it was the last time she ever did.

The fact I wasn't like any of the women here with their lithe bodies and spray tans didn't bother me. I didn't watch my calories or worry about what a man would think if he saw me naked and I had a little extra weight on my body.

Self-esteem issues hadn't been an issue for me because my grandmother had drilled into me that every *body* was beautiful. *I* was beautiful, even if I didn't fit into the mold society had created.

And no one would ever tell me any differently, not with words nor looks.

When Tara finally looked at me and saw my glare, her shoulders pulled back and she gave me a saccharine smile.

"I just couldn't do it. Without my weekly manicures, my Netflix, and then of course, ordering out." She lifted her nose in a very snubbed-up way. "I would just die." She acted and sounded overly dramatic as she steered the conversation back to "safe" ground.

I was getting a little defensive about the entire trip, because the truth was a part of me thought I was crazy for going there alone.

But the bigger part of me said I needed this. Over the last month, since my grandmother had passed away, I felt like I was in this hamster wheel. I just kept going round and round with no end in sight.

My routine was exactly the same. I went home to an empty one-bedroom apartment, woke up, went to work, grabbed takeout, and sat alone in my living room staring at the TV that played reruns.

I felt like my life was draining away right before my eyes and there was nothing I could do to stop it.

At least before I could visit my grandmother. We'd have Sunday dinners together, or we'd take hikes in the woods close to her house. Even at the ripe old age of eighty-five, she was still so adventurous.

So yeah, I was afraid, but I was more excited because I wanted to reconnect once more with the wilderness, which was something my grandmother instilled in me to appreciate and love.

I also wanted away from everything and everyone that reminded me I was utterly alone now.

"Couldn't you just go somewhere close?"

"I could. But this is where I want to go."

I'd been camping plenty of times while growing up, but never anything as intense and off the beaten path as what I planned at the end of the month. Nevertheless, excitement filled me.

"I'll be fine."

With one more veiled look in my direction, Tara muttered something about having to get back to work and left me alone.

I glanced back down at my phone, once again looking at the town of Ketchikan where I'd be staying, checking out what shops were around, then finally opening up the map that showed me the cabin where I'd spend most of my time.

I found a smile curving my face.

For the first time since my grandmother had passed, I actually felt... happy.

Maybe this was exactly what I needed to dig myself out of that dark hole.

CHAPTER

THREE

Marcella

One month later

I let the last bag I'd hauled up to my room drop
to the floor, shut the door behind me, and
looked around the tiny place I rented at the
Bed-and-Breakfast for the night.

I was out of breath from trekking up the deck
stairs that led to the entrance of my room. Sweat
beaded my brow, and I unzipped my jacket, cast it
aside, and was regretting wearing an extra layer
underneath.

But I'd read up when I was researching for this
trip that the weather up north could be finicky,
especially when I stayed at the isolated cabin in the

woods. And I was pretty sure I'd over-prepared with the amount of supplies I'd brought.

Then again, could you really over-prepare anything for my kind of trip? I'd rather take the whole kitchen sink than realize I'd forgotten something.

I landed in Ketchikan just that afternoon and took a ferry to the town where the Bed-and-Breakfast was located. As tired as I should be from the long flights—one from Colorado to Seattle, then another to Ketchikan—I felt pretty energetic.

I walked through the living room, past the kitchenette, and glanced out the window that overlooked the town. There was a bay right below and I smiled as I watched an otter pop its head out before continuing its swim.

From my vantage point, I could see the little shops that lined the streets. There was the main bridge off in the distance where a couple of older men were fishing.

Even though it was August, in this part of the country, the weather was overcast and chilly enough to where I was glad I'd brought my fall clothes. The nights would be colder, but I'd come prepared, even if lugging all that shit had been a pain in the ass while traveling.

The cruise ship was at the port in the distance, and I let my gaze linger on the horizon before turning and taking in the room, pleasantly surprised at how homey and comfortable the space was.

There was the living room and kitchenette, which were combined into one area, and the single bedroom and bathroom were down the hall.

There was only one entrance and exit, the door in front of me leading out the back of the house where there was a deck and hot tub. And then that led off to the stairs that descended to the street. And all around the B&B was a thick, lush, green forest.

I walked over to my first bag, and crouched to open it up. I only pulled out what I'd need for tonight and tomorrow morning because first thing in the morning, I was heading to the cabin, anyway.

Then I went to the rest of my bags—three in total—and double and triple checked the contents inside before zipping it all back up.

One bag alone held all the food I'd need for my time at the cabin, the other one had camping gear like battery operated lanterns, flashlights, and a radio. I also got an outside shower to hang up since there was no running water. Because a cold shower was better than nothing.

I'd been told there were pots and pans at the

cabin, as well as a wood-burning stove, and a few bundles of firewood. But I wouldn't worry over the fact I'd never tried to light a fire in my life.

I ended up bringing non-perishable foods with me. But for the fresh things like fruits and vegetables, milk and eggs and all that, I planned on stopping at the small grocery store I'd seen on the way to the B&B.

Although I was solo on this trip, I packed a hell of a lot, far more than I probably needed, but I'd rather be prepared than screwed.

I rested for a bit and walked into town, where a small restaurant was located. I wasn't much of a fish person, but I figured when in Rome and all that. So I ordered the local fish and chips and a glass of red wine.

After that, I walked around for a couple of hours, looking at the little gift shops. There was a lot of Russian influence on many of the items I came across, as well as handmade pieces of art being sold.

I made a mental note that when I came back from the cabin in five days, I'd get my souvenirs then.

After wandering around a bit and stopping by the cruise ship that was docked, I headed to the grocery store and started making my way down the aisles. I only got enough food that fit in the basket. But I grabbed two bottles of wine, because... wine.

I checked out, but wasn't in a hurry to get back to the B&B. Although I was exhausted and my feet hurt from all the walking I'd done today—not just since I'd been in Ketchikan, but also while traveling —I enjoyed the peaceful surroundings.

Everything here was so easy-going, peaceful, and clean. No smog, no cars honking, no people screaming at each other. There was no chaos, which was something I dealt with daily living in an over-populated area.

I made my way over the main bridge in town and saw two elderly men leaning against the railing with fishing poles in their hands. They were bickering with each other about the weather, one saying it was perfect for fishing, the other complaining it was too cold for them to bite.

I passed a woman who walked leisurely, her baby wrapped up against her chest as she carried a shopping bag in each hand.

Maybe one day, when I didn't have bills to worry about, when I felt more stable in my life, that's when I could make this place my home.

Because for the first time in a long time, I actually felt like I belonged somewhere.

CHAPTER
FOUR

Marcella

I clutched either side of the tiny boat, my nails digging into the icy metal as I was being taken to the isolated cabin.

I was pretty sure the boat wasn't made for choppy ass ocean water like this, but when I had voiced my concerns to Harmond, the older gentleman who was taking me, he just grumbled that it was fine and left it at that.

Of course, the day I took this trip it was a shit day with frigid rain that felt like little needles as it contacted my bare skin.

The waters were almost violent, and the boat was out in the middle of nowhere, bouncing aggres-

19

sively. I was two-seconds away from having to lean over the edge and throw up my breakfast.

The rain jacket I wore kept me mostly dry, but it didn't keep out the icy chill that even in August seemed to surround me.

My three large waterproof bags sat on the inside of the boat, the rain pelting the rubbery coating that covered them.

A wave of nausea rose in me as we went over a large crest, the boat bouncing up and down so hard my ass ached.

I started shivering, my teeth chattering as the wind and rain whipped all around me. My fingers were numb because I hadn't let go of the sides of the boat since sitting down.

I stared at Harmond. He had a perpetual scowl on his face, but I was pretty sure that's just how he looked.

Deep lines and grooves etched his face, he had white whiskers all over his cheeks and chin, was missing a few teeth, and although I knew he wasn't smoking right now given the rain, he kept his pipe wedged in the corner of his mouth.

When I'd met him at the dock, he'd been wearing a scuffed up and dirty yellow rain jacket, black rubber boots, and, of course, that pipe that had smoke billowing out of it. He'd offered me a life-jacket, ordered me to put it on, and then did the same.

We'd been traveling for half an hour before he finally acknowledged my presence. He tipped his chin and grunted, the rain pelting his face.

"What?" I shouted to be heard over the engine of the boat.

Harmond grunted again and pointed behind me.

I looked over my shoulder and squinted through the gray surroundings to see the little cabin coming more into focus the closer we got. And when we were about ten feet from the dock... the fucking rain let up.

Of course, I silently said to the sky as he maneuvered the boat, tied it off on the wooden post of the dock, then climbed out.

I glanced at him, then at the island, which was still a far distance from where we docked.

The dock bobbed as he moved around on it, the width only about four feet as he started pulling my bags out.

I was a little confused why we weren't going straight to the island when I spied a skiff off to the side.

"Can't get closer," he grumbled out, as if he heard my thoughts. "Boat will get stuck."

I knew nothing about boats or sailing or any of that, but the skiff was half the size of the boat we were currently on, and I could see the rocky beach and how shallow the water was around the island.

Harmond said nothing as he took one of my bags and transferred it to the skiff. He gestured me forward, and I unsteadily climbed onto the dock.

The platform bobbed up and down with the current and I reached for the banister, feeling my thigh muscles tense as I tried to keep my balance.

He climbed into the second boat and I took a seat next to my bags and across from him. And then he rowed us to the shore.

I learned he was a man of very few words, but got his point across through his expressions and grunts.

Once we were on the shore, I got out and grabbed my bags. He was already throwing the bags to the dock before I even set them on the ground.

"Monday at eight in the morning," he grumbled out, reminding me of when he'd pick me up to head back to Ketchikan.

"Okay. Thanks, Harmond."

He was already rowing away before I finished

saying his name, and I lifted my hand to wave goodbye despite his back was to me.

I stood there until I could no longer see him, when the fog seemed to roll across the ocean, and obscured anything farther than one hundred and twenty feet from the island.

Then I continued to stand there as I looked around. There was another smaller island right across from where I stood, and another skiff that was overturned and laying a few feet to my side.

Behind me was the cabin with a set of stairs that led up to the small deck.

I could make out a narrow wooden boardwalk that wrapped around the side of the cabin and disappeared around the back.

There hadn't been many pictures online when I booked this place, and had basically just shown the exterior of the hunting cabin and surrounding wilderness around the property.

I lugged two bags up to the cabin and set them down so that I could punch in the code to the lock and open the door.

I stepped inside and immediately the scent of age, unused space, dust, and a hint of mold filled my nose. To my left was a tiny kitchenette and a wooden two-person table.

To my right was what I assumed was supposed to be the living room, with an out-of-date patch-work loveseat, and a small coffee table in front of that held a few magazines that looked like they had been printed twenty years prior.

And the one bedroom was in front of me.

The bathroom was outside. Meaning it was nothing but a literal outhouse.

Normally the no running water nor electricity might have deterred me, but I was in a place in my life right now where having nothing but a roof over my head and no one else around was the escape I needed.

This was camping, which I was more than used to.

I quickly went out and got my third bag, hauling it inside. I shut the front door and stared at the lone bedroom, the door partially open so that I could make out what looked like a bunk bed with no mattresses.

The lone window in the room looked foggy, the glass old. I used the sleeve of my raincoat, still wet from the weather, and moved it along the glass, smearing some of the dirt away so I could see outside a bit more.

I could see the outhouse directly across from the bedroom window and wrinkled my nose.

Nothing like looking outside and seeing where someone relieves themselves to get your day going.

I left the bedroom and started going through my bags, setting the food on the table, the portable stove and the propane canisters I'd bought in town onto the counter, and putting the rest of my "electronics" on the table.

I brought my clothes and sleeping gear into the bedroom and walked back out into the kitchen to set my toothbrush and any kind of bathing items in the sink.

Since I still had my outside gear on and the rain had let up, I set up the outdoor shower and took a walk around the cabin.

After filling up the bag with the water in the large plastic rain-catching container—something I was thankful the renters had included in the "amenities" description—I hung it up and walked along the "boardwalk" that ran the perimeter of the cabin.

Because of the recent weather, the forest looked more like a rainforest, with water dripping from the leaves and the scent of earth and moisture filling the air.

The boardwalk only lined the back and sides of the cabin. The outhouse was directly behind it, and there were a couple of manmade trails leading off into the woods.

Making my way back to the front and toward the shore, I walked the waterline and listened to the sound of the gentle lap of waves. There were snails stuck to the rocks, and fish creating ripples as they jumped above the water before diving back into the ocean. When I kicked a rock, I jumped back, watching a crab scurrying away, its home being disturbed.

Tomorrow, I was going to take the skiff to the island and do a little exploring.

After heading back inside, I unpacked my drawing pad and sat at the table. Despite not having any service, I still got my cell out and pulled up some music.

And then for the next hour I sat and drew, and found peace I hadn't felt in a really long time.

I started sketching my grandmother's face, then added flower detailing. I drew hyacinth for the framework, and wisteria behind her profile.

When my hand cramped, I shut off my phone and set my pencil down, realizing I heard abso-lutely... nothing.

It was the first time in my life where there wasn't the sound of the neighbors down the hall screaming at each other, or horns blaring outside my window.

I inhaled deeply, not smelling car exhaust or pollution or somebody burning something on the stove next-door. Sure, there was age and a musty smell in the cabin, but I'd take that over all the polluted scents I was used to back home.

I rested back and closed my eyes, thinking for the hundredth time since arriving just yesterday that I wanted to live here, just burrow in deep, nestled away from everyone, and pretend like nothing else existed.

FIVE

Marcella

Scratch-scratch-scrape. Scratch-scratch-scrape.

I pulled my sleeping bag up to my chin as I stared wide-eyed at the bedroom window. I'd been hearing that sound for the last ten minutes.

There was something outside the cabin, something big walking around the perimeter, its nails scraping over the boardwalk.

My mind said it was most likely a bear, which I knew there were plenty of in this part of the world before I'd made the trip. But a part of me had clearly been naïve in thinking I'd never come across one.

The footsteps were heavy, intermittently stopping as if the animal were checking out something before it resumed. And then I heard it come closer.

Scratch-scratch-scrape. Scratch-scratch-scrape.

I white-knuckled the hell out of the sleeping bag. I'd bought a bear repellent air spray in town, not sure if it would even work, but I'd been so tired when I went to bed last night, I totally forgot to grab it and keep it close.

No amount of videos I'd watched online about taking precautions and being safe on this trip could prepare me for living it.

And then the *thump-thump, thump-thump* of its footsteps came closer before an enormous shadow passed across the bedroom window.

Oh shit. Oh shit. Ohshitshitshit.

I held my breath, pulled the sleeping bag up so that it completely covered my face and only my eyes were visible, and stared out the bedroom window.

That pane of glass wouldn't keep anything out, especially a big ass Alaskan bear. Could it hear my heart racing? Oh God, couldn't predators scent their prey's fear?

I squeezed my eyes shut as I heard the big beast right outside the window, yet not coming close enough that I could make anything out. It was too dark, the shadows too thick.

I knew sleep was most definitely not an option tonight.

I was in a cranky mood and felt like shit as I shuffled out of the bedroom and veered right into the kitchenette.

The inside was cold as hell with the early morning frost lining the outside of the windows. Last night had been an epic fail of trial and error in lighting the wood-burning stove; but after far too many attempts, I finally got it working.

I grabbed a few pieces of cut lumber and got to work, starting another fire to warm the place up. Once it was going, I sat down in front of it and wrapped my sleeping bag fully around myself.

I was seriously rethinking this entire trip. After the bear incident last night, I realized I may have made a spur-of-the-moment decision regarding coming here without fully thinking it through.

I had no way of communicating with anyone if I needed help, and nobody would know if something happened to me until Harmond came and picked me up.

But despite worrying about all that, the fear I

felt last night, and the reservations on what I'd actually been thinking about coming here, I was determined to make this the best experience possible.

Once I'd warmed up, I made a pot of coffee on the stove and sat back in front of the fire, holding the aluminum black and white speckled mug between my hands.

Falling back asleep after I heard the bear outside had been impossible. In fact, right now I was having serious reservations about stepping foot outside even if it was daylight and I was pretty sure it would be asleep by now.

But I couldn't stay in the cabin my entire trip, and I didn't want to be a prisoner while I was here, so I finished up my coffee and grabbed a quick breakfast. I got dressed, slipped on my red hooded peacoat, and then hesitantly opened the front door.

I peeked my head out but saw nothing destroyed, and when silence greeted me, I felt a little braver and stepped outside.

Because it was still early, the temperature was rather chilly, and I zipped up my jacket and put my hands in my pockets, stepping off the deck and rounding the corner of the house.

Again, I stopped and listened, but heard nothing, so I took the couple of steps it required to get on the boardwalk and made my way across the platform. Slowly.

Looking around the corner, where the bedroom window was and where I heard the bear most active, a part of me expected to see a large furry beast there, but it was empty.

I exhaled in relief, but felt my brows pull down a bit as my confusion rose. Moving closer to the window, I crouched down, reaching out and letting my fingers trail along the deep grooves that were etched into the wood.

They were big, deep and only something with sharp ass claws could create.

A shiver moved through me that had nothing to do with the temperature, and I stood, keeping the cabin to my back as I looked into the woods.

I was about to head back inside when I saw a trail that certainly wasn't manmade. It flattened the foliage, as if something enormous had trampled through it.

God, this was an awful idea.

Yeah, there was no way I was exploring today.

I kept close to the cabin, only venturing as far as the shore in front. And as the day progressed and there were no signs of any bears, I felt more at ease.

I walked along the shore, saw seals in the

distance as they popped their heads up before dipping back down.

I kept close to the cabin as I looked at all the wildlife and flora. There were so many types of mushrooms and fungi, and I'd been stupid enough to touch one, which resulted in my fingers burning afterward.

Note to self, keep your hands to yourself.

I saw mussels scattered along the edge of the water, their black shells shiny and clumped into bunches.

When I finished exploring, I sat in front of the fire pit and read for a while. The later it got, the chillier the air became, and I buttoned up my jacket and snuggled into it a little more, not quite ready to head inside and call it a night.

I stared off into the horizon, watching the sun sink down, the sky turning pretty shades of blues and oranges, pinks and yellows.

I only stayed out long enough that the sun almost disappeared in the distance before I rose and finally went inside. Although I felt comfortable and safe enough as the day progressed, the last thing I wanted to do was be outside at nightfall.

And the later it got, the more my anxiety rose. I remembered the bear outside the window. And because of my nerves, I finished half of one bottle of wine. And what do you know? That anxiety faded.

I fixed myself some dinner, settled into the small dining room chair, and used the battery operated radio that I'd brought to listen to some music. Figured I might as well get use out of it and not drain my cell battery, even if it didn't have a signal.

I had a couple of lanterns on, with one on the table and another over by the couch. There was plenty of lighting, seeing as the cabin was small.

I was in the middle of my book; the scene getting especially spicy when I heard what was clearly two animals fighting right outside the cabin.

Knowing the wilderness enough from camping with my grandmother, I knew it sounded like two raccoons. Those feral, crazy little fuckers could get scrappy when they were fighting over a crumb of food.

They only went at it for a couple more seconds and after the silence descended, I went back to my book.

I heard them scurrying across the boardwalk around the house, their little nails scraping across the wooden planks.

I could hear them run off into the woods, the foliage being disturbed in their haste to escape. I leaned back in the chair to finish my meal when I felt the hairs on the back of my neck stand on end.

As if my body was working automatically, I lifted my hand and rubbed my nape, looking around for the source that had me so uneasy suddenly.

But I was alone in the cabin. And the longer I sat there, my muscles feeling tense, the more I realized I was letting it all get to me. I was making myself terrified over nothing.

Sure, there'd been a big ass bear outside the cabin last night, but it wasn't unusual. I expected it when I came to Alaska. I just couldn't shake this strange feeling that there was something... more.

And I didn't know what exactly that was.

I finished eating and read another chapter of my book, and then got ready for bed.

I'd bathed and washed my hair before leaving Ketchikan, but tomorrow I'd brave the outdoor shower, as well as maybe taking the skiff across to the other island.

When I settled on the bottom bunk bed, I brought the sleeping bag up to my chin and lay there staring at the wooden frame of the top bunk. I didn't think I'd be able to fall asleep despite being exhausted.

All I could keep thinking about was the bear outside the cabin and it coming back.

Focusing on that lone window again, I felt my body relax on its own the longer the silence stretched out. Maybe sleep wouldn't be so elusive tonight.

Drinking that wine wasn't such a bad idea after all.

CHAPTER
SIX

Wolf

I could smell her. So sweet. So mine.

I could hear her breathing, even and slow. She was deep in slumber.

And that's why I went closer, that's why I broke in.

Although I cared little whether my female knew what I was doing, I didn't want to frighten her. If she saw me, she would be terrified.

She'd run from me.

And as much as I wanted her to do that, as much as I wanted to chase, pin her to the forest ground, and rut between her thighs like the nasty fucking beast I was, I wanted her running because she knew how much it turned me on and she was desperate to please me.

Breaking the lock on the door was easy, as easy as snapping the bones of a rabbit I intended to eat. Human contraptions were nothing but flimsy tools they thought could keep the nightmares away.

My body was too big and wide to clear the entrance, and I had to twist and shift my shoulders in order to clear it.

The cabin smelled like age and musk, like human males who'd come and gone from this place. I snarled at the thought of my female anywhere near another male. I'd rip their throats out for even thinking of her.

But underneath that old stink was the sweet scent of *her*.

I inhaled deeply, feeling desire settle right in my dick, the heavy length hardening. I followed the scent of her and stepped into the small enclosure where she slept soundly. And for long moments I just watched her, my mouth watering for a taste, saliva dripping from my fangs and jaw because she made me starved.

I looked around the small room, noticing a large bag on the floor. I moved toward it, the heavy *thud* of my feet, and the scrape of my claws on the wooden floor loud enough I expected her to wake from it. But my female slept on.

I crouched onto my haunches and curled the tip of a black claw around the small metal hook that kept it sealed, pulling it open to reveal its contents. I reached inside and picked up the first item I touched, a soft piece of fabric that smelled enticingly like my female.

Slowly swiveling my head back toward where she slept, I brought it to my snout and inhaled deeply, the scent of her pussy faint on the cotton.

I felt my cock become fully erect, a bead of seed lining the tip.

When I stood, I still held the piece of fabric, envisioning the material cupping her pussy.

My mouth watered, and I moved closer to her, curling my paw tighter around the material for a second before letting it drop to the ground.

I saw the same metal piece hanging from her covering and reached out to pull it down, like I'd done with the bag.

The *zzz* of the two halves of material coming undone had the predator in me growing more anxious. And when I pulled the top piece away from her, it gifted me with the sight of her lush body.

"Mmm," I growled, not caring how loud I was.

She was covered from ankle to chest, but I could still make out her curvy body as her clothing fitted to all that womanly perfection.

Her thighs were nice and thick, and all I could do was imagine that the female who was mine would need meat on her bones to handle the primal fucking I'd give her. I couldn't have a mate who was all skin and bones, not with how big and strong I was. I'd break her in half.

Her belly was full and rounded, and her hips wide—so that all I could picture was gripping on to them as I forced her to take my too gigantic cock.

My shaft was hard, the thick knot in the center growing as I envisioned all the filthy things I'd do to her once I had her back in my lair.

Gripping my shaft, I tightened my hold around that swollen girth. The knot was a primal part of my anatomy that would lock inside of her so I could pump her full of my cum. It would ensure I wasted no drop.

I couldn't help but imagine her tiny body under mine as I pistoned in and out before finally feeling her walls clamp around me as she found her release. She was so much smaller than me, like a little bird.

I groaned at the vision my mind conjured up of

her pussy tightening. That's what would push me over the edge and into my own carnal ecstasy.

I pumped my paw faster and harder. Every muscle in my body was tight, and I had to open my mouth slightly to get enough oxygen.

Holding in my growl of pleasure was torture, and as much as I wanted her awake so she could watch me pleasure myself in front of her, jerking off at the sight of her sleeping was a turn-on I wouldn't deny myself.

My big, hairy balls tightened with my impending orgasm, and I kept my upper body hunched over as I gripped the wooden frame above me with my other hand. My claws dug into the wood and I hissed through my fangs.

The *slap slap slap* of my paw moving swiftly over my ribbed shaft was obscenely loud, which only fueled my need to come even more.

And when she breathed out softly and turned her face toward me, I couldn't hold in my purr of pleasure.

I felt the ridges that lined my cock become more pronounced as my pleasure rose. I felt the crown swell, and glanced down to watch a thick, white drop of cum spill out of the slit at the tip.

With my focus back, lowering my gaze to her

ample tits and watching as her nipples stabbed through the material, pushed me over the edge. I came, feeling jet after jet of milky white seed spray out of my cock and coat her cotton-covered breasts. I positioned my dick so I could mark her full belly and thick thighs, needing her to be covered by my cum so she smelled only of me.

A growl rumbled from me. It was low and deep, but not loud enough she'd wake. I dug my claws even deeper into the banister of her sleeping plat-form, scraping them down slowly so they left deep grooves.

The pleasure was endless, but this wasn't about getting off, even if it felt incredible. This was about marking the female I'd deemed as mine.

This was about making her smell like me, so all other predators would know I took her and if they so much as came close to her, I'd rip their throats out.

I squeezed my paw around the crown of my cock, pushing out another drop of seed and angling myself so a thick line of cum dribbled out of the tip and covered her mouth. For a second, that single rope of cum connected us.

Oh, she was perfect with my seed painting her, and even prettier when I reached out with my oversized paw and ran a digit over her mouth, smearing it into her plump lips.

I leaned in, her curvy body so much tinier than my beastly form. She was so soft, all smooth skin and dark waves spread out around her.

Her breath moved along the fur of my neck, smelling like fermented berries. My mouth watered to see if she tasted as sweet.

I ran the tip of my snout along her cheek, scenting her, my cock hardening all over again. *So perfect.*

I didn't deny myself as I let my tongue move along the side of her face, tasting my little human female.

There was no more waiting. It was time I finally made her mine.

Marcella

Too much wine.

That was the first thought in my head as I woke and gave a groggy groan, a pounding already present behind my eyes. In fact, that's what woke me up.

I rolled over and snuggled underneath the sleeping bag further, the early morning chill in the air like a bite to my exposed skin.

But as I shifted, my clothes tugged against my skin, scratching at me uncomfortably. And then there was the tightness around my mouth as if something had dried on it.

I felt my brows lower in confusion as I unzipped

the sleeping bag and pulled the top away, looking down at my body.

At first I saw nothing, but upon closer inspection I could see parts of my thermal top and bottoms had some kind of dried substance on them. I reached out and picked at it, the material stiff.

I ran the digits along my mouth, feeling some substance covering them.

"What the hell?" I ran my nail over a spot on my thermal top, the tip scraping over whatever had dried on me. "What *is* that?"

Whatever this shit was had a distinct scent to it. It wasn't unpleasant, just... strange.

After getting up, I braved the chill outside to use the bathroom. I probably would have made the world record for holding my breath before entering that outhouse.

Once back inside, I heated some water and took a quick bath. But calling it a bath was very generous, as it was just me cleaning the important bits and any part of my body where that weird stuff had been on my clothes and seeped through.

Once dressed, I scrubbed out my thermals and let them air dry over the deck banister outside.

I still had a slight headache from the half bottle of wine that I drank last night, but despite the minimal hangover, I probably had the best night's sleep I'd had in quite a while.

I had heard no creatures outside, or I'd been too out of it to hear them. But I was feeling more optimistic and courageous today, and decided I'd save the island trip across the way for tomorrow.

Today I was going to explore those trails that were behind the cabin.

After eating breakfast, I gathered up my gear, put on a pair of long pants and some thermals underneath, and laced up my hiking boots. Then I slipped on my red hooded peacoat.

I even found a tiny basket in the cabinet, and would use it to collect some flowers to dry out so I could take them home. And then I was off, rounding the back of the cabin and going to the first trail.

For the first hour, I stayed close enough to the cabin that I could still see it. I brought my sketchbook with me and doodled some of the natural flora I came across. The mushrooms, the wild berries, the wildflowers in all their vibrant colors.

I even found a black raspberry bush that I'd been able to snack on as I sketched.

I'd had to take my coat off as all the walking around had worked up a sweat, and finally went back to the cabin to grab some lunch before I trekked back into the woods and took the second trail I'd seen.

This one was a little rocky with a steep incline, but it led me to a gorgeous creek. I spent a good chunk of time there, continuing to sketch and even feeding crumbs of my muffin to a squirrel that was courageous enough to get close to me.

I'd been outside most of the day and lost track of time, and before I realized it, I was quite a way from the cabin and the sun was setting.

The temperature had dropped considerably and so I buttoned up my coat and put my hood on as I held the basket. I collected more wild black raspberries and decided I'd eat them with dinner tonight.

As I started making my way back, I realized I had wandered further off than I intended. Although I was still on the path, I could no longer see the cabin.

I glanced up at the sky, the waning sunlight peeking through the tops of the trees, casting shards of light.

Everything had since dried from the rainfall, and I could hear birds chirping overhead, and small wildlife scurrying around me.

I glanced at the ground to watch where I was going. Boulders, pebbles and debris from the weather scattered across the clearly unused trail.

And then I felt this tightening on the back of my neck, this prickling sensation that had me lifting my hand and rubbing my nape.

I stopped and glanced around, unsure what I felt, but knowing there was something out there. But there was nothing around. Despite that, I still felt this uneasiness of not being alone.

My heart was racing, my body knowing something I didn't, that instinctual survival part of me was urging me to move quicker.

So I picked up my pace, feeling as if I were being watched.

A twig snapped in the distance, a flock of birds scattering overhead. I was panting now, running, my haste causing me to trip several times.

The heavy sensation around my body increased, and when I glanced over my shoulder, expecting to see something following me, my foot got caught on an exposed root, taking me down.

I fell onto my hands and knees, the little basket dropping out of my grasp, my sketchpad and the berries scattering all over the place. I made a gasp of pain as pebbles dug into my palms, but I pushed the discomfort away and got back up, running again.

By now the sun was swiftly setting, dusk

covering the sky. Because I was in the woods, everything seemed more ominous, more shadowy.

Stupid. Stupid. Stupid.

I should've been paying more attention, especially with the bear activity the other night. I only focused on getting back to the cabin, not caring about the basket or berries or even my sketchpad that was now left behind.

And then I heard it... something moving toward me. It was picking up its pace, twigs snapping under its heavy footfalls.

Whatever was there was huge, and all I could see was some big ass black bear charging toward me, starving and ready to tear me apart. Involuntarily, I gave out a startled cry and heard the creature move even faster. I was crying now, my vision becoming blurry.

And then it huffed out, made this deep, rumbling sound that was far too close.

I screamed when I felt something reach out and touch my hair. No way was I going to slow down or look behind me. Fuck that.

"Running only excites me," I heard it whisper.

I felt my eyes widen. Oh God, it wasn't an animal. It was a man. He was stalking me, chasing me.

And when I felt something skate down the length of my spine, I screamed again and went down hard, my ankle twisting, my body falling to the side and right down a small drop-off. I lifted my arms to brace myself from the impact as I rolled.

When I landed on the bottom, a harsh breath left me. I was dizzy, my body sore from the fall, and for a moment I couldn't move as I panted. But then I heard twigs snapping far too close for comfort and forced myself to roll onto my back and pushed myself up.

And then I saw what was several feet from me. I crab walked backward as the creature came closer. That wasn't a man. That wasn't even human. *How did it speak, then?*

My lungs burned as I hyperventilated.

The creature was wolf-like, but... not. It was some monstrous animal/human hybrid that was plucked out of my damn nightmares.

It came closer, his body hunched over as it walked on all fours.

When the thick trunk of a tree stopped me from retreating, I wanted to scream, to fight back. But I was terrified, unable to move, this cold dread washing over me.

When it was a few feet from me it stopped, the

shadows of nightfall shrouding too much of this beast. I could make out its massive body and inhuman head. I could see a longer face and a snout, sharp teeth, and fur covering its entire body.

And then the thing slowly rose to stand on two hind legs, its calves angled like a wolf's so they looked bent.

It came closer, the ground vibrating from how powerful its steps were. The thing had to be at least seven feet tall, completely covered in fur, with bulging, massive arms, hands that were more like paws and tipped with black claws. It had a thick, furry tail that was moving back and forth, reminiscent of a predator about to pounce.

God... the thing was *naked* and aroused, and what hung between its legs was massive.

"No," I whispered and shook my head, holding my hands out like that would actually ward it off.

I trailed my gaze up its barreled chest and to its wolf-like face.

Holy shit.

Although it looked like a wolf—*werewolf,* my mind whispered—it held very clear intelligence behind its dark eyes as it watched me.

"Oh God. Please. Please don't hurt me." My voice was whisper-thin. I wasn't even sure I'd spoken the words aloud. "W-what are you?" It was so close now that all I smelled was this wild scent that clung to it.

Here was this primitive creature crowding me, breathing on me... refusing to give me space. It was going to eat me. I was sure of it. Why else would it be here? What other purpose would it have for me?

"I'm the one that is going to make you mine."

I shook my head and lashed out, raking my nails along his chest, feeling hard, defined muscle underneath. He was fast as he snapped his paw out and curled it around my wrist, my palm and fingers so tiny compared to his.

I felt my survival instinct rise as I screamed and kick out, but I was like an annoying gnat compared to him, I was sure.

And when he let go of my wrist to grab my ankle, stopping my foot from connecting with the huge thing he had between his legs, I screamed again. But this time it was in fear. Bone-chilling fear.

He stood and started dragging me away like I was a damn sack of potatoes.

I twisted my body, clawing at the ground, dirt digging underneath my nails. Tears made my vision blurry, and then the world turned as he lifted me up and threw me over his shoulder.

For a second, the wind left me in a rush when

my stomach connected with his shoulder. I lay there, flopping around from his movements.

He picked up speed, forcing me to grip the long, dark fur that covered him and hold on. I sobbed uncontrollably.

"Don't worry, female. I'll have you crying for a far different reason soon enough."

EIGHT

Marcella

When consciousness slowly came back to me, I instantly realized I wasn't alone. I didn't open my eyes, just continued to act asleep because everything came rushing back, letting me relive a nightmare.

Being in the woods. Feeling as if I weren't alone. Then being chased by that—that—*thing*.

I repressed my shiver of fear as the image of the creature slammed into my mind. It was a literal monster, and the only thing I could think about was that it only wanted me for a meal.

How I wished what had been chasing me had

been a bear, because that was less frightening than whatever creature had taken me.

I could hear it close by, and the very ground beneath me vibrated slightly every time it took a step. I tried to note my surroundings while I laid absolutely still. The last thing I wanted was for this beast to know I was awake.

Whatever I was on was soft, but I could feel things scratching at my skin. The blanket—I assumed that's what it was—that covered me, smelled funny and was heavy and warm, feeling almost like velvet against my skin.

I realized, although still clothed, I was no longer wearing my boots or my jacket.

The heavy shuffling sound became louder... closer, and involuntarily I tensed. I tried like hell to feign sleep, but there was no getting around how absolutely terrified I was, and how that showed outwardly.

And then came the huffing. Puffing. It felt like hot air was moving along my arm.

The monster inhaled deeply as it dragged that inhuman furry snout along my limb and up to my throat.

I clenched my eyes tightly and couldn't hold in the whimper that left me when I felt the warm, wet feel of what I assumed was its tongue licking at my neck.

"You wake," the creature said in a harsh tone that was deeper and scarier than anything I'd ever heard. "You don't have to open your eyes for me to enjoy this."

I whimpered and tried to move away subtly, but a low growl rumbled from it and it gripped my upper arm. The beast's touch wasn't painful, but it certainly was one that told me I wouldn't get away.

It licked my neck, then ran its nose, which— good God felt wet—along the spot it had just licked. I shivered, and it hummed, clearly liking that reaction from me.

I clamped my back molars when it slid its massive hand—paw—God, whatever the hell it had, down my arm. As it came closer, I could feel the fur covering its entire body.

The thing was huge, and it used its hold on me to jerk me back toward it. I felt tears slip down my cheeks.

The scent of it was strong, a mix of pine, wilderness, musk, and something almost familiar.

"Keeping your eyes closed won't change the fact you're here with me and mine."

I could hear its voice right beside my ear, felt the deep vibration settling into every single part of me.

I realized then what that familiar scent was. It had been in my room. I gasped, shock filling me. This thing had been stalking me and had watched me sleep.

"This isn't a dream, Little One, so you may as well open your eyes and see your fate."

I didn't obey right away. I just kept my eyes closed and wished all of this away, told myself this was a bad dream and that I'd wake up and be back in the cabin.

But the way it kept running its big, furry paw up and down my arm, and the gentle scrape of its claws along my exposed skin, made it impossible to focus on anything else.

I kept replaying the image over and over again. This wasn't a human behind me. I didn't know what it was.

I slowly opened my eyes so I could fully grasp the reality that I was now in. Although the creature was behind me and couldn't see my face, especially with all the darkness and shadows, it purred as if pleased I had listened to it.

I wanted to tell it to fuck off, but when it slid its paw over my hip and placed it on my belly, its palm was so massive that it encompassed my entire abdomen.

The urge to squeeze my eyes shut again and just block all of this out was strong, but when it jerked me back toward its massively huge body, my mouth went slack at the feel of something hard, long, and *huge* pressing against my lower back.

I made a startled sound and tried to move away, but its clawed paw was still pressing on my belly, keeping me in place with zero effort.

"Hush now, my little female. I have no intentions of using this—" he rolled his hips forward, digging what was clearly an enormous erection against my body "—on you until you beg me for it."

I shook my head, biting my tongue because I wanted to scream that I'd never want him or *that*.

And then it curled its big paw around the flesh of my belly, squeezing it, and letting out what could only be called a purr.

It moved to my hip, doing the same to the flesh there before releasing it and slipping down to my thigh. The creature curled its palm around my upper leg, giving it a little jiggle before growling low.

"Your body is perfect."

My mouth dried, and I felt something move through me. I couldn't describe it, but hearing him praise my form in that totally inhuman voice made me feel hot and tingly in places that had no business feeling that way.

I was in that weird mental state of processing its words when suddenly its big paw was covering my breast. I squealed out when it gave the mound a squeeze at the same time it thrust against me, digging that steel rod into my back and pulling a gasp from me.

"Do you like the feel of your mate?"

My heart was jackhammering in my chest. *Mate? The fuck?*

It was pure instinct that had me slapping his furry paw hard enough I felt his entire body tense. I realized I may have just screwed myself over.

Before I knew what was happening, I was flat on my back with this beast hovering over me. I'd known and felt how massive he was well before now, but having him crowd me like this had me feeling minuscule.

I shrank back from his wolfish face when I spied the rows of sharp teeth in its mouth.

"What are you?" I whispered, horrified.

"I'm yours," he said with finality. "You are my female, and I am your male."

I shook my head, denying what he said.

It—*he*—placed his hands on either side of my body, caging me in with all that muscle and fur and unworldly appearance.

It was hard to make out the details of what he looked like because the cave, which I assumed we were in, was so dark. But when he lifted an arm, I flinched.

With my eyes shut and my head turned, I expected a strike. When nothing came, I slowly opened my eyes and tentatively looked back to see him staring down at me, but I couldn't read his motives.

He looked between me and his raised paw and then back at me. I could imagine his brows—if he even had any—lowering in apparent confusion.

"What is this?" He rumbled out and then slowly lowered his hand to his side. "You think I would hurt you?" His tone took me back because it was so... gentle, if that was even a word I could use to describe him. "You think I would ever harm *my mate*?" He sounded almost aghast.

There was that word... mate. I could tell just by his tone it meant a hell of a lot.

Oh God. This beast has taken me because he sees me as what, his girlfriend? His wife? His fuck toy?

When I didn't respond, he leaned back, his gaze

almost softening. It had my defenses lowering just marginally.

"I'm not yours," I whispered.

The grin he gave me was slow and almost ominous. He didn't have lips, didn't have a mouth like a human would. But the flash of his teeth once again had me laying as still as possible. All I could think about was not making any sudden moves.

"Oh, Little One, you are mine. And," he leaned in close, and I once more smelled that musky, wolf aroma that made me feel *all kinds of things*. "You have nothing to fear from me because I would kill anyone who even thought of hurting you."

I slowly lowered my arms but kept them pressed to my chest, terrified of what this creature would do, even if it was very clear he wouldn't hurt me.

For a moment I just lay there as he still hovered over me, his body so much bigger that I couldn't help but feel like this little doll beneath him.

My eyes had since adjusted to the darkness and I could actually see a little firelight flickering around his shape.

"What are you? What do you want with me?" I didn't expect him to answer, but I had to ask. I wanted to pretend like I was dreaming, thrust into some nightmare where this big sinful creature crawled out from the deep woods and snatched me away.

He cocked his enormous head to the side, his ears twitching. The creature didn't have blunt teeth, but sharp ones I envisioned he needed to tear into the flesh of his prey. Dark fur completely covered him. He had a long snout, pointed ears, and large, round black eyes.

His shoulders were impossibly broad, his arms muscular, bulging and thicker than my thighs.

I refused to look any lower than his defined abdomen, but I didn't have to notice that what he was sporting down below was huge and very hard. I snapped my gaze up to his face to see him looking at me almost inquisitively, as if he were just as curious about me as I was about him.

"What are you?" I whispered, asking again because he hadn't responded. It was a prolonged second before he huffed out a breath.

"Wolf," was all he said.

I pushed myself up and scooted all the way back until the rocky wall stopped me from retreating. After pulling my legs up to my chest and wrapping my arms around my knees, I just stared at him, trying to make myself as small as possible.

All I kept thinking was, *don't make sudden moves,*

don't make him mad. And then, on the heels of that thought, I remembered the look he'd worn when I thought he was going to strike me.

"I am me," he said matter-of-factly.

"You're not human," I stated the obvious. "What are you?"

He didn't answer for long moments, just stared at me, and I could tell by looking into his dark eyes he was highly intelligent. It was the way he watched me with this probing stare, like he could pick up every single little nuance that made me... *me,* and dissected it all.

"My kind has always been here. Since the beginning of time."

I let that sink in. Okay. So he was just different from me. Although it might be hard for some to accept that, how could I deny it when he was a living, breathing wolf-creature right before me? I hadn't seen a lot of things in my life, but that didn't mean they didn't exist.

"I am what I am." If he was the type to shrug, I had a feeling he would right now, as if what he said was the simplest of facts. "I've seen humans come and go through these parts over the decades. I learned their language, listened to the stories they told each other, and learned about their world. They would call *me* a monster, but the things I've heard these men say, the way they spoke of their females... and they are the ones that are the beasts."

I felt something tighten in my chest and it wasn't unpleasant.

I didn't know how long we stayed silent, but never once did he take his gaze off of me. He still crouched on his haunches, that gigantic body blocking the only escape. Although I wasn't stupid. I knew that even if I tried to run, he would catch me. He was a predator, that much was obvious.

"Why did you take me?" I felt like I'd asked this question a million times, but it was like he couldn't —more likely wouldn't—answer.

He made this noncommittal grunting noise before he turned and stalked toward where the fire-light was flickering.

I exhaled roughly, not realizing how much I'd been holding my breath intermittently.

I didn't know how long I sat there, assuming he wanted me to follow, but I stayed put long enough my ass felt numb. I would have stayed here the whole time if not for the thought that he'd come back in here and haul me out like a rag doll.

I was on some kind of pallet that was covered in

thick furs on top, and pine needles and dead grass underneath.

The smell that surrounded me was damp and heavily smelling of earth. Although I knew I didn't want to go out there, and didn't want to follow him, I also was very aware he'd just hunt me back down.

So I stood, knowing I should probably figure out what the hell was going on.

CHAPTER
NINE

Marcella

O nce I stood, I stayed where I was for another long minute. I was afraid to leave, to go out there and face whatever Wolf had in store.

But finally, I tentatively moved down the tunnel until it opened up and curved to the left, showing a large open area. I could see Wolf sitting before a fire, his immense body still seeming to dwarf the cavernous area.

His arms hung between his legs, his focus on the flames, and thank God the position that he was in shielded the massive erection that I had felt digging into my back. Because yeah, this girl had for sure looked.

His attention was on the spit angled over the flames as he manually turned it, roasting whatever small creature he skewered through the center.

I fought back the wave of nausea as I could see its charred body being roasted.

Although I wasn't a vegetarian, it seemed a little too crude for me, and not something I was used to seeing living in the city. Hell, back home, my meals had been presented beautifully on a plate, or I opened the bag and pulled it out before unwrapping it.

Wolf didn't look up, didn't even move, but I knew he was fully aware of me standing just a few feet away from him.

I took a few moments to glance around the cavern and check everything out. In reality, I was trying to find where the escape route was. The interior was small, with the opening about twenty feet to my right. The ceiling—is that what the top of a cave was called?—had stalactites, but was high enough that I knew when Wolf stood he wouldn't have to crouch.

I could see a stack of furs, amongst other items

like rocks, bones, sticks, a pile of pine needles, and crudely woven baskets filled with things I couldn't quite make out from where I stood.

When I glanced back at the creature, it was to see him staring at me, his black gaze trained right on me in the most penetrating of ways.

"What are you called, female?"

My tongue felt too thick to form any words and answer. I ran the muscle along my bottom lip, noticing him watching the act. "M-Marcella," I whispered.

He hummed a gruff sound. "My Marcella. Come here." His voice was growly, and a part of me felt like he said it with a gentle tone. He held out his large five fingered paw and beckoned me over by curling his claws toward his palm.

He was a monster. Literally. And I knew he had no intentions of letting me go. So why would he care if I was comfortable or not?

But I still moved toward him, instinct telling me the last thing I wanted to do was piss him off. *Survival Marcella. This is you being smart until you can get away from him.*

The closer I got to the fire, the more I felt my shivering lessen and realized I was freezing. I wrapped my arms around my middle, the chill having nothing to do with the cavern air, and it all having to do with the shock of... everything.

I kept the creature in my sights the entire time as I rounded the fire to sit on the opposite side, keeping the flames between us as if it was some kind of barrier that could actually protect me. That was laughable.

I tried to glance at the exit again, trying to be inconspicuous as I rubbed my chin on my shoulder, but I could feel Wolf staring at me.

"You can try," he said in a low voice that had me looking back at him sharply, feeling my eyes widen. "You can run." He focused back on the fire and reached up to unhook the spit and pull it away from the flames. "But you're mine and there's no place you'd be able to hide where I wouldn't find you."

My heart was thundering and I could feel it in my throat. I didn't answer as I watched him tear the carcass from the spit. His paws were huge, easily bigger than my head, and his sharp, dark claws on the end I could envision he used to slice open his prey.

"So run, my little mate." His tone was almost bored. "Run if it makes you feel better, safer, but know this—" He started peeling meat off of the animal and setting it on a flat stone beside the fire. "—that the chase only makes me want you more." He said that last part on a growl and I couldn't suppress my shiver.

Hearing that sound should've made me feel only one way. Instead, I felt something that wasn't fear.

I didn't respond because what was I supposed to say?

So I just sat there, keeping my gaze locked on him because he was intimidating as hell, and looked like someone had plucked him right out of a horror movie.

I watched him finish tearing at the flesh, and when he picked the bones clean, he grabbed the flat stone and stood. I craned my head back as I looked up at him and braced myself, my muscles tense as he walked around the fire toward me.

I scuttled back until the cave wall stopped me. He made an impatient, almost irritated sound in the back of his throat. *What do you expect?* I wanted to snap at him.

"Eat," he huffed out that one word as he stood before me, holding out the stone with the food piled on it.

When I didn't take the rock, he set it down in front of me and turned to move toward the pile of baskets. He crouched and pulled back a fur, and I realized it covered a deep hole. He reached in and grabbed something, but with the way he positioned himself, I couldn't see what it was. That was, until he turned around and I saw several—very dead—rabbits hanging from his paw.

He made his way back over toward the fire and came to sit far closer to me than I liked. And then he started tearing into the creatures. He pulled off the skins in one swift move before tossing them aside. I covered my mouth with the back of my hand and felt bile rise in my throat as my gag reflex kicked in.

Then he was eating them. Fucking raw.

I sat there just watching him devour these rabbits, blood covering his dark fur and dripping onto the floor. The sounds he made were harsh and animalistic, with growling and snarling, as if instinct dictated he couldn't eat silently.

When he finished, the bones picked clean and set into a pile to the side, he ran an enormous paw over his snout and jaw, wiping off the blood, but really he just smeared it all over.

And the entire time he acted like the beast he

was, he stared right at me, keeping his focus trained on me as he ate like a heathen.

For a moment neither of us moved, my stomach cramping from what I'd just witnessed. I was using every ounce of self-control I had not to gag at the grisly sight of him. And then there was the smell. A coppery tang that filled the cavern so thickly I felt it coat me.

Wolf slowly rose, unfurling that vast body from his crouched position as he came toward me. The fearful sound that left me was involuntary. My eyes felt so wide that they were drying out, but I was afraid to even blink. If I did, I might not see his next move.

But all he did was lower himself onto his haunches in front of me, his clawed toes digging into the dirt as he balanced himself. Wolf reached out and picked up the flattened rock with all the cooked meat on it.

He picked up a long slice of meat between two razor-sharp claws and held it out to me. "Eat." His voice was stern, the tone reminding me that I was a petulant child disobeying him.

I pursed my lips again and felt a spark of annoyance. But even if my anger was rising, my fear was still at the forefront.

"You need to eat." He shoved his paw closer to my face, and I turned my head, but still kept my focus on him.

He made a rough sound, one that was clearly a warning, and my heart started beating faster, if that was even possible. It already felt as if it were going to burst through my chest.

When he huffed out, it surprised me that the sound was almost in defeat. He lowered himself fully until he was sitting on the ground in front of me.

He set the rock between us, still holding that piece of meat out to me as if this wasn't something he'd budge on relinquishing.

"Please?" I swore I saw his forehead furrow like the taste of that single word on his tongue confused him.

The surrounding air changed, that lone word seeming so foreign to him. He almost sounded like he wasn't used to saying it, as if maybe he'd never uttered that single word before.

And I believed that.

I didn't know what made me do it, why I even cared about how he was handling the fact I was refusing anything he offered. But before I could stop myself, I reached down and picked up a piece of meat.

"I'm doing this for me, not you," I murmured. "Just so that's clear." I saw his mouth—snout, whatever the hell made up his face—slightly lift, as if in amusement.

My body told me to woman the hell up as my stomach betrayed me and growled. He made a noncommittal grunt but didn't move, just sat there staring at me. He was expectant, as if seeing me eat was one of the most important things he'd ever witnessed.

"You'll eat."

I narrowed my eyes at him.

"Because I will not have a mate who's skin and bone."

I felt my irritation grow, pushing away that fear. "Excuse me?" I all but seethed.

He leaned in an inch and bared his fangs. And as terrifying as that sight was, I strengthened my shoulders and tipped my chin up.

"I want my female to take her fill." He moved in a bit more. "I need you thick and perfect so I can hold on to something as I fuck you."

Oh holy shit. My heart beat harder.

"You understand me?"

Did he actually expect me to answer? When I didn't respond, he gave a sound of warning.

"I'll make it clear, female, I want you to eat and eat well. You'll always have your fill. You'll never go hungry." He reached out before I knew it, and his enormous paw cupped the side of my face, his entire palm encompassing me. "My sole purpose is to take care of you, and I'll do that so well you'll never go without." His voice was a husky sound. I felt it spear right between my legs.

He pulled back, and I exhaled, realizing I'd held in my breath because he affected me in ways I wasn't comfortable acknowledging.

"Because what I have planned for you, Little One," he said, and let his black gaze trail to my breasts, then along my thighs, and back to my face. I *felt* that look. "What I have planned for you makes me hungrier than I have ever been."

I could feel how fast I was breathing, could hear it fill my head and drown out all other sounds. "What big eyes you have," I whispered before I could stop myself.

"Mmm, the better to look my fill of your lush body with, my Little Bird."

"What sharp teeth you have."

He watched me like a predator. "The better to destroy anything that thinks to harm you with." His teeth looked so vicious as he dragged his tongue along them, as if he could taste me already.

Again, I felt that feeling wash over me that was confusing, yet made me want to feel more of it.

"Eat, precious," he said suddenly, snapping me out of my thoughts and pushing the feelings that were curiously strong inside of me away so I was once more thrust back to reality.

I exhaled a shaky breath and brought the piece of meat to my mouth, telling myself it was just food. To escape, I would need my strength.

After eyeing the string of meat, I popped it in my mouth and started chewing, pleasantly surprised at the flavor. It was a little on the gamey side, and was tough as I chewed, but the flavor was good and I realized how hungry I really was. I took another piece.

He leaned a little forward, and I moved back. The sound that came from him wasn't one I could describe.

But I felt, strangely enough, that it pleased him I was eating.

Before I knew it, I'd eaten half of the meat strips that were on the rock.

Wolf gave a grunt and stood, moving over toward one side wall before bending down to pick up what looked like a water bladder.

He turned and came back toward me, and against my better judgment I glanced down, expecting to see a massive dick swinging between his legs.

But it surprised me to see... nothing.

No, that wasn't accurate. I could see his large, heavy balls, and above those was a massive, furry bulge.

And the longer I stared at it, the more I saw things changing. I felt my eyes widening as he started getting aroused, his dick coming out of that bulge above his sac.

My mouth went slack as the seconds ticked by. A part of me should have been disgusted by what I saw. But the truth was I clenched my thighs together because heat settled right at the center of me.

And then he was completely erect. His cock was human-like, but not.

Wolf's girth was as thick as my wrist, and the length had to be half of my forearm. His foreskin hung over the crown of the head slightly, but I could make out the outline of the crest underneath. And he was already dripping copious amounts of pre-cum that fell to his muscular, furry thighs.

"The longer you stare, the harder I'll get."

He was watching me with clear heat behind his black eyes.

"I have to pee," I blurted out and stood, my knees wobbling as I sucked in a deep breath, trying in vain—and failing—to act like I didn't just watch his dick come out of that furry pocket above his huge balls.

Apprehension had me edging away from him and toward the cave entrance, my hands on the rocky wall behind me. Because the truth was, I needed something to keep me stable and grounded.

But he wasn't letting me put too much distance between us as he followed me out, his still hard cock bouncing slightly from his steps.

Once at the mouth of the cave, I turned and took a few more steps away from it before stopping and sucking in a lungful of the chilly night air. A shiver moved through me. I tried everything to feel a semblance of normalcy again.

Have I ever really felt "normal"?

I could feel Wolf right behind me, but I didn't

turn around. His presence was the most tangible thing I'd ever felt.

I wrapped my arms around my waist, the act an involuntary reaction that had nothing to do with the chill, and everything to do with how I heard him come closer, how I found his body heat blanketing me.

How I smelled that familiar scent that I couldn't quite place until...

My pulse picked up as the realization finally settled in me. I had to tilt my head back so I could look into his face, and before I knew it, Wolf was lowering his upper body so his face was right in front of mine.

His nostrils flared as he inhaled deeply, and I swore he smiled.

"You were in my room," I whispered. "The way you smell... it was you."

He didn't respond, didn't deny or confirm it. He let me go after I took a step back.

"I saw you. I wanted you. So I took you," he said again, so clearly, so matter-of-factly, it was infuriating.

"There's this little thing called consent, Wolf—"

The sound that left him had the rest of what I was about to say dying on my tongue.

"Say that again."

Was he serious? "Fuck you, buddy." Again, he made that sound, and I felt the vibrations all the way through my body.

"Say that again, too." His teeth flashed as he smiled. The bastard. "In fact, say them both in the same sentence. Say, 'fuck me, Wolf'."

"You're a beast and a pervert." I felt my eyes widen as the words spilled from my mouth on their own.

His eyes became hooded as he inhaled again.

"Why do you do that?"

"Do what?" He was staring at my mouth as he asked the question.

"Keep... smelling me."

His gaze slowly trailed back up my face so he could look into my eyes. "Because your scent is so good, Little Bird. Your pussy smells so sweet when you get wet."

My face felt like it was on fire.

"I'm not... I'm not aroused." I swallowed the thick lump in my throat and moved a step back. He followed me.

"Mmm, you forget I can tell when you're lying." His gaze lowered to my lips. "And the scent of your frustration over the fact you're turned on because of me makes your scent even more addicting."

Could he hear how hard my heart was beating? It sounded like war drums in my ears.

"You asked *why* I took you, and I told you because I wanted you, but maybe you need to hear it a different way." He reached out, and I was so frozen in place I let him touch me, let him cup my cheek again and smooth the pad of his thumb over my skin. "When I saw you, I knew you'd be mine. Your body was made to handle the fucking I plan on giving my mate. Your curves and thickness were created to carry my big pups."

My pussy tingled. The traitorous bitch.

I felt the gentle scrape of a deadly claw move down my temple and I sucked in a sharp breath.

Because it felt good.

"I've never wanted anything more than I do you." I felt his warm breath brushing along my face and neck.

He leaned in again, and I felt a stream of air along the shell of my ear, the wet sensation of his nose moving against my cheek.

I didn't know why I did it, but I closed my eyes and shivered. It should have disgusted me that Wolf was so close to me, touching me. But when I felt something warm and wet slide along the side of my face, and heard him rumble low, I couldn't stop the arousal that suddenly claimed me.

I also couldn't stop the little moan that slipped past my parted lips.

He was licking me, dragging his enormous tongue along my face and tasting me. I felt my pulse beating right between my thighs.

Wolf pressed against my body, his fur thick but soft. The tips of my fingers tingled, urging me to reach up and touch him. I didn't know what was wrong with me, why I wasn't screaming and crying and trying to escape right now.

But Lord help me, I didn't want to move. I didn't want him to stop.

And so I didn't move, and instead leaned in closer, lifting my hands, and just as I was about to place them on his chest, curling my fingers into his fur, he took a step back.

It surprised me at how... disappointed I was at that.

When I opened my eyes, he made this sound deep within his chest. Was he... was he laughing at my reaction? My cheeks heated, and I gritted my teeth as I tried to push the embarrassment away.

But when I stared into his face, I saw nothing

but that stoniness he wore so well. I noticed his nostrils were flaring and his chest was rising and falling.

He was affected. The same as I was.

I looked at his jaw, neck, and finally his chest. I felt that nausea rise back up in me. How the hell had I forgotten he was covered in blood?

Was I so starved for any kind of attention that common sense and my survival instinct had suddenly taken a back seat?

He held his paw out to me and I stared down at it, but didn't make a move to give him my hand, which he obviously wanted.

He gave a frustrated growl and was the one to take my hand then, his touch still gentle though. Wolf held my palm in his and the sheer size difference between us... amongst other things, startled me all over again.

Everything about Wolf was magnified.

As a bigger, curvier girl my entire life, I'd never felt "tiny". Not that I ever wanted to be. This was how I was made, and I embraced the hell out of it. But right now, looking up at this seven-foot beast, I felt minuscule. Breakable.

And why did I feel turned on because of that?

I let him lead me through the forest, the night so

thick that it was impossible for me to see anything. So I had to trust him, even if I had no reason to.

We didn't walk very far from the mouth of the cave before the sound of babbling water broke the silence. Although I felt exhaustion over everything, when we broke through the clearing and I could see a small trickling waterfall that led to a generous pool of water, which then continued downstream, some of my tiredness faded.

My body ached from running and trying—and failing—to get away from Wolf. On top of the fact I'd fallen a few times in the chase and was pretty sure I had some nasty bruises hidden under my clothes, I felt this almost serene sense being out here.

I wasn't afraid despite the thick darkness surrounding us, and predators nearby. How could I when Wolf stood a foot from me and all I could keep remembering was him telling me he'd destroy anything that thought to hurt me?

There was this ethereal sort of glow being cast along the top of the water, and a cool breeze took that moment to brush over me, moving the tendrils of my hair along my shoulders.

I was so lost in thought and appreciation of the view that I didn't realize Wolf was urging me down to sit on a large boulder at the water's edge.

For a second I just looked up at him, and there was this strange heaviness that seemed to surround us as he stared right back at me. He made another sound, a series of grunts and purrs, before he turned and headed toward the water.

I'd wondered more than once if I was dreaming. Because all of this was just too unrealistic to be life. But it felt real. *He* felt real.

Curiously, I watched him walk toward the water and get in, moving toward the center. He didn't face me right away as he started washing himself off, droplets splashing around his body, his dark fur almost looking black now that it was wet and plastered to his body.

I could clearly see how muscular and hard he was all around. Huge, broad shoulders, long arms with bulging biceps, and forearms that were cut and defined and had me clenching my thighs together.

He might not be human, but he was the most masculine, powerful thing I'd ever seen in my twenty-two years of life.

I glanced around, realizing I could try to sneak off while he wasn't looking and preoccupied. I even braced my hands on the boulder and was about to push myself up. But I knew... knew that it was pointless. At least right now. I needed to be smart, because if I tried escaping now, he'd only catch me, and then his defenses would be up.

I had to lower them, get him to think I was submissive to his ways, so he wasn't on guard. And then I'd try to leave. That was the sane thing.

And when he turned around, I couldn't help the sharp breath I sucked in. The bastard was getting erect. I watched in a strange sort of awe and fascination as his cock emerged and he reached down to wrap his big, meaty paw around himself. And the longer I stared, the harder he got. His huge, hairy balls started swaying slightly as he jerked off right in front of me.

I shouldn't have stared, but how the hell was I supposed to *not* watch as he pleasured himself? It was clear he was a damn exhibitionist.

I guess that made me a voyeur, because my pussy was soaked watching him masturbate. With the moonlight casting a silvery glow over his body, I really stared at his shaft.

So long. So thick.

And because he was so damn hard, every time his palm moved up to the base, I could see these raised ridges all along the length.

Built-in ribbed for her pleasure? Well, damn.

He also had a swollen ring in the center of his

cock, one that I could see throbbing even from this short distance.

My throat was so damn tight and my mouth so dry. I tried like hell to stop watching him, but the sounds he made, the grunts and groans coming from his chest, told me he liked me being a creep, apparently.

How could I call him a pervert when I was doing the same things?

He slid his palm down to the tip, then moved it back up, pulling at the foreskin so I could see the thick crown of his cock underneath.

I could make out the way his tail flicked back and forth, lightly splashing the water as if he couldn't help himself.

Cum was steadily dripping out the wide tip, and I realized the slit had to be that big because this creature probably came like a damn geyser.

My pussy seemed to like that—especially as I envisioned all his cum shooting out as he got off—because my inner muscles tightened on their own. It was almost like my body wanted something big and thick shoved up deep inside.

Oh my God, I was a nasty bitch, insane as well. Who got horny thinking about a wolf creature coming all over the place?

87

What type of person got kidnapped and had a wet pussy at the very idea of wrapping her hand around that monster of a cock and seeing if her fingers would touch?

Me. I was that nasty bitch, and I wasn't even fighting it.

CHAPTER
TEN

Wolf

My Little Bird thought I didn't see her looking for an escape. Did she not understand there was nowhere she could run where I wouldn't follow?

Did my Marcella not fully realize there wasn't a place she could hide where I couldn't find her?

Her scent was fully ingrained in me. It was a part of me now. And the sooner she came to terms that she was mine, the more pleasure I could give her.

And I wanted to give her an immeasurable amount.

But I let her have this false bravado, this faux idea that she could outrun me. I was a wild, primitive beast, mind and body, and my instincts were brutal and attuned for survival.

And now that I had my Marcella, I was even more so. Because nothing would take her away from me, even my little mate fighting this.

I would just have to show her how good it was with me, how well I would treat her. She would be my queen, *my* alpha. I would worship the ground she walked on and would make sure she had everything she could ever want.

I just wanted her to realize that she was mine, and I was never letting her go.

And when I felt her watching me again, my cock hardened, lengthened. I wrapped my paw around my shaft and gave it a good couple of strokes.

It felt good to jerk off, knowing she was watching me. It was incredible to smell her arousal and all the sweet nectar that spilled from between her thighs.

Thick strings of my cum spilled from me, flinging into the water, becoming even more prominent as my desire grew.

But I wanted her to see *all* of me. I wanted to see her eyes widen and her breath catch as I stroked myself and really came all over the place, spilling my seed into the water like I'd do on her body, in her mouth... deep in her womb.

"Come here, precious." She still sat on the boulder, but I could hear her blunt human nail scraping against the rock.

I could see the way she clenched her thighs together, how her breathing picked up.

She stared at my erection. I let her look her fill as I palmed myself. I held the heavy length as I dragged my palm up to the crown before sliding back to the base, pulling the foreskin down so she could see the bulbous, swollen head where my seed continuously dripped out.

I watched as she bit her lip, her little white teeth a stark contrast to the red flesh, and I could see the flush that made its way from her face, down her neck, and disappearing under the fabric that covered her tits.

I wanted to suck on them, wanted to watch them get bigger, rounder, dripping with milk as she grew heavy with my pups. And I'd lick those full, dark nipples, lapping up the sweet liquid that would spill from the tips and feed and nourish our children.

"I said, come here, Marcella." My voice was husky and serrated, the primal side rising and wanting to just go to her and make her do what I wanted, to show her that her hesitance wasn't needed.

Even if it turned me on like a fiend.

Did she know that the fire she spit at me only aroused me further and made my cock ache?

She slowly rose and made her way toward the water's edge. When I brought her to my lair, I wanted to undress her. I wanted to tear the material from her body and feast my eyes on all that perfect flesh.

As I stared at her slit, I imagined gripping her thick thighs and wrenching them open.

My mouth watered, saliva dripping out of the corners as I growled low and pictured dragging my large tongue through her pussy lips.

I knew she'd be sweet and musky and taste like *mine*.

I waded closer until she was only a foot from me, my cock still in my hand as I lazily stroked myself.

"Grab hold of me." I stared at her. "Stroke me until I come all over your hand." I tipped my head down but kept my gaze locked on her.

She sucked in a sharp breath and shook her head.

A burst of amusement filled me. "My Little Bird thinks she has a choice."

She parted her lips and dragged her tongue over the full bottom one. Marcella hadn't taken her focus off my shaft the entire time, and I could feel even more pre-cum seeping out of the slit and sliding down the underside of my dick.

"I shouldn't want anything to do with this."

She sounded as if she were talking to herself, but I could smell how wet her pussy was. I wanted to bury my snout between her thick thighs and lick her cunt until she gave me all her sweet honey.

She stood at the water's edge, and it would take no effort to just pull her in and hold her tight as I moved to the center where she couldn't reach the bottom.

She'd have to hold onto me. I'd get to feel her big tits pressed to my chest. She'd be forced to wrap her legs around my waist. Even now, I could see the hard points of her nipples stabbing through the material that shielded the mounds from me.

My mouth watered as I thought about tearing the flimsy fabric away and nosing her, smelling her, and finally fucking her.

I wanted to trace the heavy mounds with the tip of my nose as I inhaled deeply, scenting her. I bet

93

she had big, dark areolas that I wanted the shade to deepen from her arousal.

I growled at the image of that. My cock jerked at the thought, and my balls drew up.

"Take hold of my huge cock and stroke me, Little Bird."

She looked into my face then, her pupils blown out from her desire, the scent of her drenched pussy saturating the air between us. There was no hiding that she wanted me to fuck her, but she was still fighting it, still trying to deny the ending that she'd find herself in, regardless.

"I can't—"

"—You can and you will." I reached out and took her hand, and brought it to my dick. I made her wrap her fingers around my length.

Her palm was so small that it didn't even wrap around half of my girth, but I kept my palm over hers and forced her to stroke my cock.

She was panting now and intermittently shaking her head. The way her eyelids fluttered told me she was trying so hard to fight this.

"Just give in," I hummed, and started moving our hands over my length faster.

She still shook her head, but she kept her gaze locked on where I made her touch me.

A soft sound left her, and I groaned as I moved her hand lower, curling it around the crest so she could feel how much she made me drip with pre-cum.

Her rapid breathing fueled my arousal. We started working our hands over my stiff cock even faster. I wanted to touch her so badly, to curl my palm around her massive tit and just squeeze, feeling how soft she was, how much she'd mewl for me because she'd love the feel of me touching her.

I stared into her face the entire time, unable to look away as she watched both of us jerk me off. My cock was throbbing, the thick vein on the underside pulsing, the ribs circling my shaft hardening.

"Can you imagine me thrusting this deep inside of you?" I stroked us faster. "Can you picture how good it would feel to make you take all of it, to feel these ribs throbbing in your pussy, touching every part of you?" My knot throbbed as I envisioned shooting my load and filling her with my seed.

I rumbled low, groaned harshly, and picked up our speed. She made an almost distressed sound, and I realized I was squeezing her hand too tightly, but I couldn't help it with all my wild passion.

"I'm going to touch you, Little Bird." I didn't wait for her to give me permission, just reached out and curled my hand against her waist, jerking her forward, the water splashing around us. And never once did I stop our hands from stroking over my shaft.

I slid my hand up to the underside of her breast. She was breathing so hard that the mound was bouncing slightly, the weight heavy.

And then I molded my big palm around the fleshy mound.

I leaned in and dragged my snout along her throat, over the underside of her chin, and followed the same path with my tongue.

Fuck, I was close to coming, and adjusted my body to the side so I now faced her, my cock pointed right at her belly. I wanted to make a sticky mess on Marcella so she'd never be able to clean it fully off.

"Marcella," I growled and bared my teeth, a warning for her to obey me.

She exhaled and slowly tipped her head so she could look into my face.

"You'll look right at me as we do this, as I claim you this way for the first time."

I squeezed her hand with my paw, knew I was probably hurting her, but she didn't tell me to stop. And even if she tried to stop this, I couldn't. I was too far gone in my primal need to have her, to make her see and feel and fucking *know* that I'd never let her go.

"Wait," she gasped out, but I just curled my fingers tighter around hers. "I can't do this."

"You will do this. You're going to get me off so I can come all over you." She made a strange noise and halfheartedly tried to pull her hand back. And although I kept my hold on her, if she truly wanted me to stop, I would have let her go.

She wanted to act like she needed this to stop, but I could smell how sweet and drenched her cunt was. I could hear her little mewls that she tried to keep buried deep in her throat.

Her pupils were blown, her lips swollen and red because she kept biting them.

I slid my paw over her nape to tangle my claws against the back of her head, gripping the strands and jerking her head back.

"Are you going to be a good girl and admit you're mine?"

She moaned again and shook her head, which had me humming in pleasure and frustration at her defiance.

And when she mewled out, when she closed her eyes and parted her mouth even more—as I smelled her orgasm flower in the air—that's when I let myself go.

I let a low rumble leave my chest as my balls tightened, and I exploded, spraying my seed all over her belly before angling my cock up so the thick white ropes splattered against her throat.

She gasped.

I pulled her in closer and dragged my tongue along her mouth, repeatedly. And still I kept marking her because she was mine.

It was a second of me sucking in great lungfuls of air, my body shaking and shuddering from getting off, before I felt calm enough to think clearly again. Jerking off wasn't foreign to me, but I'd never had a female touch me. Until her.

While she was still in her post-pleasure haze, I didn't stop myself as I dragged my tongue along her cheek and then over her lips again. When she parted her lips, I let my tongue slip in.

I didn't have a mouth or lips, and could never kiss her the way I'd seen humans do. But I could lick her, lapping at every inch of her body until she shook and cried out for me to give her more.

"You," she finally said in an almost shocked tone before that surprise faded, and I could see the spiciness I loved so much in her come forth. "It was you."

She glanced down and picked at her shirt, my cum soaking the fabric and I felt fierce pride because of it.

I knew she'd figured it out, and my length started hardening again at that reality. I *wanted* her to know that what I'd done was something my kind did when we found our mate.

"Say it, my fierce little female. Tell me what you've realized."

She took a step back, and I let her.

Her hands were curled into tiny fists at her sides, her nostrils flaring, the scent of her annoyance filling my nose in the most tantalizing of ways.

"You... you..." she couldn't get past that lone word, but I didn't move, didn't speak, just watched her and let her work through this.

"You came all over me like a damn pervert."

I moved a step closer, the water rippling around me. "I *marked* you."

The sound that came from her was loud and shrill. "Marked me? Like a damn dog pissing on a tree?"

I cocked my head to the side. "No. Like a predator, I am making sure anything and anyone who comes close enough to scent you will know you're mine." I snarled, the very thought of another male even looking at her having rage filling every part of me. "My scent covers you, my sweet Marcella, and it's that smell that will let any other predator know that I'll shred them apart if they so much as touch you."

I moved another step forward, and her survival instincts claimed her as she retreated one back, causing a high to fill me as the predator I was rose, as well.

"You came all over me," she said again and blinked, her lips parting. "Marked me." She whispered softly those dual words as she looked at the water.

I bared my teeth in the only form of a smile I could give her. "I did, and you look gorgeous covered in my seed." If I could have laughed, I would have at the anger she threw my way. But I grabbed my cock, which had gone hard in an instant, and started stroking myself all over again, "I can give you more, if you like?"

She made a frustrated sound and turned, storming off toward the shore, and I hummed low in pleasure.

My mate was a force, that was clear, and I hungered to see how much I could push her.

CHAPTER
ELEVEN

Wolf

Before we'd made our way back to my lair, Marcella had washed as much as I allowed, because what I refused to let her do was clean off my seed from her clothing. She'd huffed, puffed, and threatened to "kick me in the balls".

But I'd just smoothed my palm over the side of her neck, down her tits, and over her belly. When she realized I was further rubbing in my cum, she said a few more colorful words in response.

And it made my cock thicken all over again.

After that, I'd taken Marcella back. The fire had been nothing but embers, and after I added a few more pieces of wood to make sure it stayed warm enough in the cave for my little mate, I'd told her to go to our sleeping pallet.

My fiery female had crossed her arms over her chest, kicked up her cute chin, and pursed her lush, pink lips at me before telling me to "fuck off".

Didn't she know this push and pull from her turned me on?

I let her sleep as I prowled the outside and made sure there weren't any other predators stalking my territory. I'd called this lair mine for so long anything that had a brain and wanted to survive knew to stay away.

But I wouldn't take any chances with my tiny mate. I'd made sure my warnings were seen and smelled and known loud and clear. Body parts of the creatures who'd dared cross onto what was mine had met their end and left to decay as a warning.

I urinated on the trees surrounding my cave, letting my scent saturate the air, dragged my claws over the thick trunks so the gouges would show all, I would do the same to their bodies.

I started making my way back to my Marcella.

Once back in my cave, I made sure the fire was good for the next few hours. I didn't need the light or heat, but I'd always be prepared for my little human.

She wasn't built like me, with thick fur or heightened senses. I'd have to be careful with her and stay attuned to her needs.

I grabbed a bladder of water and made my way to our pallet, set it beside her in case she woke and was thirsty, and then just stood there staring down at her.

A thick fur covered her, and the steady rise and fall of her chest told me she slept. I got on the pallet, pulled the furs back, and slipped in behind her so I could curl my body around hers. I wrapped my tail around her belly, the thickness adding warmth to her. And when she reached down and buried her hands in the thick tuft of fur, I hummed in pleasure that she sought me out.

I buried my snout in her hair and inhaled deeply. Having Marcella with me made me feel more content than I ever could have imagined. I never realized how lonely I'd been until I saw her and knew she was mine.

The stiff length of my erection dug into the soft swells of her ass. I didn't stop myself as I ground against her, rolling my hips. A low hum of need tore through my chest and I gripped my mate's generous hip, squeezing gently as I pulled her back against me.

And still she slept, so exhausted that she didn't even wake. As I scented her, I kept my snout buried in her hair, wanting her branded by me.

I kept rolling my hips back-and-forth, holding her tighter, her ass so full that when I pushed against her a little firmer, my cock pushed against the crease of her leg coverings.

I groaned and pushed the hair away from her neck so I could look at her, drag my tongue over the side of her throat and thrust back and retreat.

Mmm. I wanted to pull her pants down just enough to reveal her ass and feel her warmth.

And so I did just that until she was bared for me.

Marcella moaned slightly, still sleeping, but popping her ass out and telling me how much she wanted this. I pressed forward and felt her cheeks part as my cock nestled in the warm crease.

She was perfect. She was mine.

I kept pumping my hips forward and dragging my long, thick shaft up and down the crack of her ass. A snarl of primal desire filled me when my dick head brushed against her pussy slit and I felt all that slick honey already coating her cunt.

She hated she wanted me, but couldn't deny she

ached for more. Her body wept for me, and the very idea of lifting her leg, throwing it over my hip, and sinking in deep was so strong I tightened my hold on her and picked up my pace.

That she slept on but her body instinctively reacted to me, knowing I'd take care of her, was such an aphrodisiac I knew I'd orgasm again.

I growled, curling my hand in front of her, slipping it between her legs and lifting it up slightly. I adjusted myself so my cock slipped right between those juicy thighs, the warmth of her body, and the slickness from her pussy, making my motions easy as I glided back-and-forth.

I grabbed her fat tit in my paw, feeling how tight her nipple was as I squeezed the mound and picked up my pace, throwing my hips back-and-forth.

My cock slid in and out. In and out.

And then I came, exploding, spraying cum everywhere. She moaned again, her body shattering. My cock was now nestled between her plump pussy folds and rubbing against her swollen clit.

Even in sleep, she came for me. I opened my mouth and gently locked my jaw on her throat, not hard enough to break the skin, letting her know I was the one in control.

I wanted her to be spread out before me, naked

and willing. Her thighs parted, her pussy soaking and primed for me. I wanted every inch of her covered in my marks. Bites and scratches, bruises and seed.

She'd look so perfect like that.

When I was spent, my seed smeared between her thighs, I relaxed on the pallet and pulled her in close.

She stirred, moaning again, and pressed her bottom to my groin.

"So pretty." She had dark hair, and I smoothed my claws over it. I brought the strands to my snout and inhaled, rumbling in pleasure at her scent.

I knew when she was fully awake because her body stiffened against mine and she slipped her hand under the furs, no doubt feeling all my creamy cum covering her.

"You motherfucker," she murmured, her voice still slightly sleepy, but there was no heat behind her words.

I bared my teeth and gave a huff—a chuckle.

The sooner she realized I was a nasty beast for her—only her—the more orgasms I could give her.

CHAPTER
TWELVE

Marcella

Two days. That's how long I'd been in this cave with Wolf.

He'd watched me like a hawk, following me wherever I went, touching me anytime he was close enough.

And every night he forced me to sleep beside him, would touch me... pet me slowly and gently, stroke me between my legs until I shook and came. He didn't try to fuck me. And I was shameless in admitting every night when I was on the precipice of going over the edge, I'd almost beg him to put that monster cock inside of me.

I glared at him over the fire as he skinned and

107

prepared a rabbit he'd brought back after he went hunting.

I'd tried escaping then, but I hadn't gotten more than five minutes from the cave before I heard him roar out. Running had been almost laughable. He'd caught me moments later, tossed me over his shoulder like a bag of laundry, and spanked my ass hard enough I'd stilled from the shock.

So here I was, glaring at his big, furry body as he sat there, oblivious to my annoyance. The scent of copper tinged the air, and I should have been gagging, but the other scent, the one of cooking meat coupled with the sound of it sizzling, had my stomach growling and my mouth watering.

"For you," he grunted, and tossed a small cloth bag toward me.

I eyed him warily before reaching for it and opening it up. Inside was an assortment of berries and nuts, some I'd never seen before, others I recognized when I picked during my hike.

The polite side of me wanted to thank him, but the annoyed part—which currently was a hell of a lot stronger—had me grinding my teeth together, and instead set the bag aside.

He kept working on the animal, but I could see

he watched me intermittently out of the corner of his eye.

"I know you think you're keeping me," I said in an even tone. You caught more flies with honey than vinegar, my grandmother always used to say. But I also knew Wolf didn't give a shit about any of that. He had to be the most stubborn... creature I'd ever met in my life.

"But I'm supposed to meet a boat on Monday. If I'm not there, they'll come looking for me."

He didn't respond as he started opening up the animal with one of his black claws. I held in my gag reflex at the sight of the blood oozing out of the gaping wound. And then he just started pulling out entrails and tossing them aside.

"They won't find you." His tone was stoic, as if this was the most pointless conversation he'd ever heard. What a strange thing to realize, given the fact he wasn't even human, and it wasn't like he had anything else to do.

Wolf cut off pieces of meat and started cooking them over the fire. And although I knew he liked his raw, he never ate before me after that first time. He waited until I got my fill before he ate.

I hated and loved how that made me feel, how it softened my heart slightly toward him.

But the truth was if I took away the fact he kidnapped me and was holding me hostage—which were pretty big damn cons in his corner—Wolf had only ever taken care of me.

He made me his priority with shelter and warmth and food... and, of course, pleasure.

Nightly, he'd taken me to the pond where we'd wash and he'd all but rip the clothes from me to wash them. He didn't care that I told him—demanded—he take me back to the cabin, and if he did, I'd have more of a variety.

I stopped bringing it up when he said he'd much rather I go naked.

It had only taken me two days of having to wash in the pond like an animal, and of course, watching him touch himself in the most obscene manner, before I'd quickly gotten over being self-conscious. It was all just skin, right?

And what was the point of caring about that kind of stuff when, in the grand scheme of things, it didn't matter?

Besides... Wolf was very adamant about touching every inch of my body and giving me at least two orgasms before he let me go to sleep.

He'd slowly remove my clothing, run those big furry paws over every inch of me, growling low and in a way that had my pussy so wet it was embarrassing the effect he had on me. Then there was the whole jerking off like an obscene bastard as he watched me. He got off on being an exhibitionist.

As I imagined that, I felt my face heat.

I cleared my throat. "You don't care if anyone comes looking for me? What if they find us and capture you to do crazy experiments or something?" At the thought of that, my stomach went sour and my heart started beating a funny tempo.

I didn't like the thought of someone hurting him.

"Let them come," he grumbled out and turned the meat, the continued sizzle of it cooking on the rock overly loud. "If they are smart and clever enough to find my lair," he said slowly and looked at me. "And think they can take you from me..." he paused, his voice ominous. "They can fight me and see if they win." His voice dropped lower. "They won't. But they can try. I'll rip their heads clean off their necks and feast on their blood."

He went back to cutting off strips of meat, his mannerisms like what he'd just told me was everyday conversation.

I stared at the fire, lost in my own thoughts. I reached up and started braiding my hair, something

I'd been doing the last two days to keep the tangles at bay.

In fact, I'd had to resort to really roughing it up in every aspect. Brushing my teeth with mint leaves he brought me, using sand along the edge of the pond to scrub myself before rubbing my skin with these pungent leaves he gave me, which I guess acted like soap.

When I glanced up, he had his gaze locked on the motion of me braiding the locks.

"Will you teach me?" His deep voice had my thighs involuntarily clenching. I was like Pavlov's dog when it came to him. Just a rough growl from Wolf and my pussy perked right up.

"You want to learn to do my hair?"

He grunted and gave a nod of his boxy head.

"But why?" I felt my brows pull low in confusion.

"I want to care for you in all ways, and that includes ensuring you don't have tangles."

Oh God. There went my heart, doing that funny beat in my chest again.

I glanced away, my face burning. I hadn't blushed so much in my life. "Okay," I whispered, not allowing myself to look at him because I knew that would cause my brain to turn to mush and any self-control vanish. "I'll teach you." I closed my eyes and breathed out.

A long pause filled the cave, and I focused on the fire again before I tried one last time.

"Will you take me to my cabin?" I glanced at him again. "Please? I want my things. My sketchbook and pencils, my clothes, my comb and toothbrush and just... all my shit, Wolf."

Although he brought my jacket and sketchpad from when I'd been running, the paper had gotten damp and torn, dirty from the fall, so was now useless. I also had nothing to draw with. And I was feeling a certain withdrawal from not being able to sketch.

"That will make you happy?"

His question surprised me, and I stared at him for long seconds before nodding. "Yes. That would make me happy." *Amongst other things*, I thought to myself.

He grunted and went back to work cutting up the animal.

"Then I'll take you where you need to go."

All I could do was sit there and stare at him. That had seemed so... effortless. Why was it so easy now, but he'd made such a big deal about it before? Wolf glanced at me as if he read my thoughts.

"I'm an alpha. I'm dominant. And I always get my way."

I refrained from rolling my eyes.

"But I can't expect you to accept the situation and me, if I'm not willing to do the same."

I blinked at his candor. Damn Wolf for making me like him a little more.

He grabbed the meat off the fire, not even acting like the heat bothered him, and brought the food over to me.

He sat in front of me, and I didn't shy away as he picked up a piece of meat and gave it a few seconds for the strip to cool off.

I just stared at him, feeling something strange grow in my chest. For being so beastly, he was this gentle giant deep down inside.

Wolf held out the food and I went to take it from him, but his low growl and a small shake of his head stopped me.

"Let me feed you." He leaned forward and focused on my mouth. "There's nothing I want more than to please you, Marcella." He was breathing harder now. "And feeding you gives me great pleasure. So open for me," he huskily murmured.

I parted my mouth and let him slip the food inside.

"That's my good girl," he all but purred. "I want you to be happy here. I want to give you whatever you need and desire."

As I chewed, my heart was pounding and my body was lighting up.

"And if it'll make you happy to gather your items, so be it. I'll take you at first light."

Wolf was changing the rules. He was going from captor to caregiver, and I shouldn't have felt myself wanting him because of how soft he was being toward me.

I knew what I'd do when he took me. Gathering my things from the cabin wasn't the *real* reason I asked again.

I'd try to escape. I knew that would probably be my only chance, because as much as Wolf took care of me... this wasn't my home.

Right?

THIRTEEN

Marcella

S nuggling in deeper under the furs, I felt my eyes droop with sleepiness.

After I'd eaten my fill of the meat strips, and the nuts and berries Wolf had given me, we'd bathed, come back to the cave, and now I heard him shuffling around.

I let that drowsiness take over just a little more until the motion of Wolf awoke me, as he pulled the fur aside and slipped in behind me.

He smelled like the outside, like the crisp air and the absence of pollution I'd been so accustomed to while living in the city.

His body was also cold, as if the wind had

stroked over his fur from being outside. I tried to move away slightly, a shiver claiming me at the chilliness that surrounded him. But he wouldn't have any of that.

He placed his palm on the center of my belly, gave a grunt of disapproval, and pulled me back against his chest.

Then he wrapped himself fully around me, his erection already digging against my ass, which immediately sent a flush of heat straight between my thighs.

Being held by him shouldn't have felt so right.

It shouldn't have felt so good or arousing. Because I was so wet right now and all it had taken was the scent of him and the feel of his body against mine to turn that switch on inside me.

I wanted more of those heavy pets he liked to give me before I fell asleep, wanted to feel him dragging that thick tongue over my exposed skin and hear him growl because he loved doing it so much.

I lay there and feigned sleep, even though I knew he was probably fully aware I was awake.

I was having a hard time controlling my breathing, felt myself become wetter, my nipples stabbing through the material of my shirt.

My clothing was stiff from having to air dry after

washing it out in the pond. I should have gone naked while I slept, the material scratchy and abrading my flesh, but my clothes almost felt like a shield, like they would somehow help me keep my sanity and not accept this as my reality.

Even if—the more I thought about it— this wasn't the absolute worst outcome I'd ever experienced.

And truthfully, I enjoy feeling his warm, big body surrounding me.

I was losing my mind. Could you get Stockholm Syndrome this early after being kidnapped? Was everything I knew about reality completely false? How could something so good and feel so right be wrong in any way?

I could feel his tail moving up and down my calf before sliding up to my thigh. He curled his paw around my hip, thrust gently against my ass, digging his cock against the crease.

I closed my eyes and bit my lip when his tail slid along the edge of my shirt, pushing it up slightly as he teased my midriff that he exposed.

An involuntary shiver moved through me and I told myself not to mewl like a kitten. I wouldn't make a sound, couldn't let him know how much I enjoyed this.

But why? Why couldn't I enjoy this? Why couldn't I just say screw everything and everyone and take this one thing for myself?

"My sweet, sweet Marcella. You feel so perfect against me. You'll feel so good once I push my cock deep into your human body and claim you fully as mine."

My head was fuzzy, euphoria filling me.

"You're the best. No other female will ever compare to you. No other creature will ever be as important as you are to me."

Don't think about anything else but how good this feels. Don't let his words and touch sway you in your plan to figure out a way to escape tomorrow.

I couldn't control my breathing then. I didn't even try. I let out a shuddering breath when he moved the tip of his tail along my hip, over my waist, and gently dragged it right under my breasts.

"Let me make you feel good." Wolf ran his tongue over my cheek, and I moaned then. "Let me strip you bare and lick every single part of you until you're writhing and begging me to finally fuck you." He kept moving his tongue over the side of my throat painstakingly slowly.

It was more torture than arousal at this point.

His tongue was just so big and foreign, and he smelled and felt so damn good.

I was biting my lip repeatedly, so much so that the flesh was tender, that pain adding to my growing desire.

And when I felt his tail move back down and tease the crease between my thighs, I shamelessly parted them and allowed him access.

I wore pants, but I could feel the gentle brush of that hairy tail sliding lower, teasing my fabric-covered pussy. I needed more.

God help me, but I wanted more.

"Let me in," he said in a baritone voice, and I made a sound that didn't even seem like it could have ever come from me. It was a silent affirmation.

Do whatever you want. Just don't stop.

Although I didn't speak, I knew he knew fully that I was completely on board with this because, in the next second, he rose and started removing my clothing.

When I was completely naked in front of him, he just crouched on his haunches and stared at every single inch of me. For so long.

But I didn't feel self-conscious, didn't feel like covering myself from his appraisal.

Because the thing with Wolf was, he looked at

every single part of my body like he was dying to touch it, to taste me, to memorize every dip and hollow, every curve and roll.

I could see in his body language that he hungered for me, and it was a powerful feeling.

"Your body was created for the rough fucking I want to give you." He let his gaze travel down to my belly. "The perfect form to carry my big offspring."

How could hearing him say such lewd things cause a visceral reaction inside of me?

Wolf reached out and started running his palms over my belly, squeezing my flesh, gripping the rolls I loved about myself.

"Look at this perfection."

I gasped as I felt electricity spear right into my clit.

He was growling, his cock so hard that pre-cum was a steady drip from the crown and sliding along the underside before catching on the fur of his thighs.

"I want you to ask me for it, beg me to make you feel good."

I hesitated, and he leaned in and bared his fangs.

"You'll do what I say because you want to please me."

I grew so damn wet.

"Now be my good girl and tell me exactly what I want to hear."

Listening to this wolf-beast throw the dirty talk out was such an aphrodisiac that I parted my legs on command.

Wolf leaned in and closed his eyes, inhaling deeply. "Your pussy is so primed for me, isn't it, my tiny human?"

Before I could respond, I saw a flash of motion beside me a second before his tail landed right between my legs, smacking my clit.

My back arched, my breasts shook, and this sound I'd never heard come from me before, tore from my throat.

"What the hell—" That last word died in my throat when he brought his bushy tail down on my soaked pussy again.

He strategically placed it so when it landed, the tip grazed my clit so sharply that an involuntary spasm claimed me.

He was making these animalistic noises above me, his paws on either side of my legs, his claws digging into the pallet.

He kept spanking my pussy with that tail until I felt tears leak out of the corner of my eyes.

I shook my head, not sure if I wanted him to stop

or keep going because the pain was leading to this incredible pleasure that had my thighs clenching, my breath stalling, and then I came for him so suddenly I couldn't hold back the scream of completion that exploded out of me.

"That's it," he said in the most primal voice that speared right into my clit and caused the orgasm to feel so much stronger. "That's my girl. Pleasing me so much by getting off for me. Mmm, your pussy is getting so wet and ready to stretch around my cock."

He leaned in close and licked the side of my face. I closed my eyes, moaning as I turned my head further to the side so he had better access.

Wolf's tongue wasn't smooth. It was rough, textured, kind of like grains of salt running against my skin.

I wondered what it would feel like between my legs as he licked my pussy and got me off that way.

And as if he knew where my thoughts were, like he could smell all that wetness spilling from my tight hole, he gave my jawline a gentle nip before he started moving down my body.

He dragged those sharp teeth between the center of my breasts, and the sensation of that sting coupled with his big wet nose descending had my pussy clenching. I opened my legs as wide as they would go, muscles stretching and pulling, but once again, that discomfort just fueled my desire.

I gasped in pain and looked down, seeing his sharp canines had broken the skin right below my belly button.

Beads of blood welled, and I watched in stunned disbelief as he leaned back just enough to let his tongue slowly unfurl before he dragged it across the redness, smearing it along my belly before continuing to lick it clean.

"Tonight, I'm finally making you mine."

And I knew the definition of what he meant by that was more wild than anything I could ever envision.

FOURTEEN

Wolf

When she parted her thighs for me, allowing access to her sweet, sweet fucking pussy, I growled in carnal need.

"More, Marcella." My voice was almost unrecognizable from my primal desire. "Spread wider and let me see the slit I'm feasting on tonight."

She opened a little more, but I grew impatient. I gripped my claws under the back of her knees, jerked her legs open—hearing her gasp—and lifted them up to press to her chest.

"W-wait," she said, and I snarled. I hated that fucking word.

"No more waiting." I tightened my claws around the back of her legs and kept her right where I wanted her. "You need me to lick this cunt and get you off, don't you?"

I let my gaze trail over her nicely rounded and full belly, over her heaving chest and big tits that shook slightly, and looked at her face.

Her pussy lips were glossy, pink, and juicy, and I couldn't help but inhale sharply. She smelled sweet and musky and everything that I didn't know could be addicting.

I'd never wanted to indulge in anything in my life, but with my mate, I wanted to gorge.

"I'm going to need to do this every night." I leaned in, rubbing my snout along her inner thigh.

Even her skin tasted good, fresh, like the water that came down the creek from the mountaintop.

Reaching up, I gripped the soft skin of her belly and rumbled in appreciation as she gave me a nice pawful.

And then I took my fill of my soft little human.

I thrust my tongue into her tiny pussy hole, forcing the thick, wide, and textured muscle inside.

She cried out and tried to push me away, but I growled in warning.

"*Mine*."

"It's too much."

I retreated to let her body get accustomed. "You'll take it all. It'll hurt. You might even cry, but you like me tongue-fucking this perfect slit. You like knowing this monster is getting you off."

I looked up the length of her body to see her eyes wide and her pulse beating frantically at the base of her throat.

"Now be my good girl and ask me to fuck you with my tongue again." She didn't answer right away, and I dug my claws into her thighs hard enough I knew I pricked the skin. I smelled the tangy scent of her blood and held back my groan.

She gasped, then... moaned.

My female liked a little pain. I could give her enough to push her over the edge so she'd soak me.

"I want that," she finally whispered, and looked down at the marks I'd given her, the scratches from my claws that had broken the skin.

They weren't deep, wouldn't scar, but droplets of blood welled along the lines. Before I could stop myself, I leaned in and dragged my tongue across them, licking at the coppery taste of her essence.

"Holy shit, Wolf. You did not just do that," she whispered, but there was no disgust in her voice.

And as I dragged my tongue across the scratch marks again, I looked in her eyes to let her watch as I did this very carnal act.

"God," she breathed out.

"Your God won't save you from me and all I have planned."

I couldn't get enough of the nectar that spilled from her pussy as I moved my tongue through her slick lips, over her swollen little clit, and finally sliding down and plunging it into her tight hole repeatedly.

I fucked her this way, and every time I pressed my tongue into her body my cock gave a harsh jerk, throbbed, and pre-cum spilled from me until I made a sticky, puddled mess beneath me.

I tightened my hold on her belly further, knowing my claws were breaking the skin, but she kept moaning, kept lifting her hips and grinding her pussy against my face.

"That's it. Rub this little pussy all over my snout, get my fur soaked so all I smell is your juices," I said against her saturated flesh, and she came for me, her back bowing off of the furs, her big tits jiggling, her nipples tight and hard.

I had my paws around those massive mounds and squeezed, plucking at the peaks, rolling them between the digits until I knew it hurt, until I felt all her cream spill out and onto my tongue.

And I drank it up, swallowed every fucking drop. I'd die if I didn't taste her every night, if I didn't have the flavor of her orgasm sliding down my throat and filling my belly.

She was still riding that high of pleasure when I gave her slit one more last long, languished lick and pulled away.

My perfect human blinked up at me with a dazed expression on her face, and watched as I palmed my cock, stroking myself and pushing even more seed out of the crest.

The way she bit her bottom lip and then dragged her tongue over the plump flesh, had me baring my teeth, saliva dripping off of my fangs because I was so fucking hungry and primal for her.

"Come here."

Marcella slowly rose, then got into position on her knees as I rose to my full height.

"Open," I demanded, towering over her.

She parted her lips and stared at my dick. "It turns me on to see all of that ribbing lining the length, knowing that the center of your dick swells when you're aroused."

I was eager to show her it not only swelled, it would also lock me inside of her.

Pre-cum dribbled out of the slit at the tip, and every time I stroked toward the crown and then moved to the base again, I pulled back the extra skin, revealing the thick, bulbous head with more clarity.

"Tell me how much you like my cock." My huge balls swayed from the force as I stroked myself faster.

I was full of cum, ready to fill my little human until it spilled out of her as soon as I pulled my dick from the tight grip of her pussy.

"I love it," she whispered, and moved closer, opening her mouth, her jaw getting wider as she slowly slipped her tongue out, expectant and waiting for me.

I brought the tip of my shaft down on her tongue, slapping the muscle over and over again, letting my semen cover the pink muscle until it turned a milky white.

"Swallow," I snarled, and watched as she gave my cockhead a lick before she closed her mouth and did as I said, drinking my cum. "Open again."

As soon as she parted those lips, I shoved my dick inside, pushing all the way in until the back of her throat kissed the tip.

She gagged, her eyes watering as she stared up at me, but she didn't back away. My Marcella gripped my thigh fur and held on as I started pulling out and pushing in, making her take as much as she could.

"You look so pretty with a mouthful of my cock."

I pumped into her a few more times, spraying more cum down her throat before I pulled out, her lips making a popping sound when the suction broke.

She'd soon find out that I could come many times in a night, and I'd show her that fact right now, as I started jerking off furiously, aiming my dick right at her face, and then exploded.

I painted her mouth and chin, her neck and her chest with milky white ropes of semen. Her tits were shaking from the force of her breathing, and I'd seen nothing prettier than my female marked by me in this carnal way.

With one last spurt across her lips, I groaned, "lick it off."

She obeyed so nicely as she ran her tongue along her lips, then gathered what she could from her face to bring it to her mouth and sucked her fingers clean.

"Rub it in." I was still hard as I watched her reach down and smooth her palms all over her skin, smearing all of me into her creamy flesh.

With a ferocious howl, I pushed her back down, jerked her legs open wide, and then slid my palm between her tits to grip her throat.

I could feel her pulse beating rapidly underneath her skin, and added slight pressure as I positioned myself.

She was so small underneath me, all pale skin against my dark fur, so very different from my beastly visage.

And I'd seen nothing more beautiful in my existence.

Her pussy was so tiny compared to my thick cock, but she'd learn to take me, and her body would become accustomed to my size.

I notched the head at her entrance and, with no warning, with no kind of extra preparation, I thrust in hard, seating myself as deep as I could. I forced her to take it all, and her cry was one of pleasure and pain.

"It's too big," she cried out, and placed her

palms flat on my abdomen, adding pressure as if to push me off. "You're just too much."

"You can handle it. You were made to stretch for me. You *will* take all of me." I tightened my hold on her neck as I eased out of her, keeping the crown lodged inside of her before I slowly pushed back in.

I did this repeatedly, letting her get used to the feeling of me stretching her.

Only when she relaxed against the furs did I slide my hands down her generous hips, gripping her tightly there, and then started fucking her raw like the animal I was.

I jerked her down on my length at the same time I thrust back up, the sound of wet skin slapping together, filling the cavern, and causing jets of seed to explode out of me.

But I didn't stop. I kept going harder and faster, riveted to the sight of her tits bouncing before I glanced down at how stretched and pink her pussy was around my dick.

"Oh God, it hurts..."

"You love it," I growled, and she moaned, nodding and affirming that she did fucking love it. "Take all of me," I snarled. I leaned forward only long enough to drag my tongue along the side of her face. "Take every inch until it hurts and you're split-ting in two."

It wasn't in my nature to go slow or be gentle. I'd never done or known such acts in my life. As a soli-tary creature of the woods, I had to be fierce and aggressive, strong and territorial. It was the only way to survive.

A part of me wanted to be sweet with Marcella, to show her I wasn't this beast that rendered flesh with my fangs or tore limbs apart with my claws.

But the stronger side of me was all primal, more dominant, and I really plowed into her, swinging my hips back and forth until the sloppy sounds of her wet pussy sucking at my ribbed cock filled my head. I heaved, wanting this to last, wanting to rail her until the sun came up.

I needed to go deeper.

Gripping one of her legs, I lifted it up, pressing the top of her thigh to her chest. I wrapped my tail around her ankle and did the same to her other leg.

Then I stared down at her cunt and fucked her brutally. "So pink. So wet. You'll be sore once I'm done with you."

I bared my teeth, making sure she was focused on me when I gritted out, "I'll fuck you repeatedly until my seed takes and you're mine in all ways."

My sweet mate, so fragile yet taking my dick like she was born for it.

I pulled out so suddenly, gripped her waist to flip her over, and pulled her up so she was on her hands and knees.

I brought my paws down on her, spanking her, watching the big mounds jiggle from the motion. And I pulled those ass cheeks apart, staring at that tight little hole between them.

"Once I've broken you in, I'm going to fuck this hole too." I smoothed a digit along the tightness, pressing in slightly before gripping the base of my shaft, lining it up with her pussy, and plunging into her body.

I bent over her, latched my mouth on to the side of her throat, sank my fangs in, and pounded into her harder and faster with each passing second. I snarled against her throat when she told me to slow down. My teeth latched on to her, an act showing her I was the dominant.

I was the one who did the fucking.

And when I felt her inner muscles tighten around me, I gave in to the need to go over the edge.

I teased her clit with the tip of my tail and felt her finally orgasm. My knot swelled, and the ribs along my length hardened. I came so hard that I had to break away from her neck and roar out my release.

And all the while I was mindful to keep playing with her clit, to keep dragging out her pleasure until I could feel our combined wetness being forced out of where we were joined.

My orgasm tore through me and kept climbing until I grew dizzy from it, until the only thing I was mindful of was the thrusting of my hips back-and-forth. I fucked my mate so hard that when I glanced at Marcella, I could see she had to brace one hand on the cavern wall in front of her to keep stable.

I leaned back to stare at where I fucked her, my cum and her pussy nectar slipping out from the sides and making a big mess beneath.

"Don't stop, Wolf. Don't stop." She kept chanting those two words, and I raked my claws down her sides, scratching her as I made my way to her ass and started spanking the cheeks repeatedly.

I curled one paw on the back of her neck, pushing her face down, popping her ass up, and I rutted between her legs like a feral creature in heat.

With one last pulse of cum shooting into her body, my knot swelled another fraction, ripping a groan from me at how incredible it felt. I stayed locked in her, unwilling to let go of this feeling.

She collapsed forward, and I wrapped my forearm around her stomach, lowering us to the pallet so that I could curl my body around her. Marcella had her back to my chest, and I slipped my tail between her legs to lift one up and keep it over my hip.

I was still buried deep in her, refusing to pull out even though my knot had decreased in size.

She squirmed in front of me, and I grunted in warning, clamping a hand on her belly and pressing her back against me

"No. You stay right there. This is how we sleep. With my cock buried deep inside of you and no chance that my seed spills out of your womb."

"You freaky bastard," she sleepily murmured.

I expected her to put up more of a fight, to give me more of that spark of life that I craved so much, but she just sighed in contentment and snuggled back against me, slipping her hand down so that she could curl her fingers around my thumb.

And I felt something tighten in my chest as I rose just enough to look down at her face. That tightness grew to an uncomfortable level, a pain I'd never experienced before.

My perfect human was sleeping, pressed against me and showing me all the trust in the world, like she knew I'd protect her. And all the while my Marcella held on to that digit.

Although I knew I'd never let her go because she was mine, this feeling growing in me was something different, and not anything I'd ever experienced before.

It was an emotion that had my heart softening toward this little thing, and a small voice inside of me moving from total dominance to something deeper and more meaningful.

As I stared at my mate, I knew *she* would be the only one to ever have control over me. And I would gladly give it to her ten times over.

CHAPTER FIFTEEN

Marcella

I felt like something had shifted inside of me from last night to today, the changing of my thought process and how I wanted things to play out.

I'd been so set on trying to escape Wolf and this situation, finding any means necessary to just get away, but I hadn't really stopped and fully appreciated that I was actually... happy spending time with him.

Sure, I didn't have my creature comforts like the internet, running water or heat, or even a proper bathroom, but I didn't need any of those things. And for the first time in my life, I didn't feel any kind of pressure to abide by rules or laws or a certain set of standards.

This was just a wild, primitive way of life, but it worked. And it felt good.

I tried to be quiet and slow as I shifted on the pallet of furs so I could stare at him. His paw tightened on my waist, as if he thought I was trying to escape. I had to be going crazy because I actually smiled and felt this warmth bloom in my chest at the thought of him being so territorial and protective of me.

For long seconds I just looked at him, memorizing how different he was from me, yet with each passing moment with Wolf, he became more familiar.

I'd probably stared at his face and took in all his strange, beastly yet beautiful features a hundred times over since he took me. But I couldn't help myself as I looked at his pointed ears, and couldn't stop myself from reaching up and running my fingers along the edges.

The fur was so thick but also soft, and they twitched slightly as I moved the digits behind them and down his face.

He made a deep sound in his throat but continued to sleep and so I kept exploring him. I touched his snout, running my fingers over the edge of his black nose, then down his broad shoulders and bulging biceps.

His chest was so hard and defined that I felt a different heat settle right between my legs. After the fucking he gave me last night, there should be no way I'd be interested in sex right now.

I was sore and sticky from the amount of cum he'd left inside of me. Yet I was ready for him to touch me, to scratch me, to give me more marks that currently covered my body.

With that thought in mind, I glanced down, pushing the fur away so that I could see my breasts and belly, my inner thighs and my hips. I was covered in red and purple fingerprint sized marks, scratches all down my sides, more bluish colors covering my belly.

I touched them lightly, not sure why I found them so beautiful. I had to be losing my mind. When I glanced back up at Wolf, I made a small sound of surprise at his dark eyes—open, and his gaze locked on me.

He looked down at where I touched my belly, my fingers circling over a rather large bruise he'd given me in his primal passion. Slowly, he trailed his gaze back up to my face, made a deep sound in his throat that I knew all too well, and he was suddenly pulling the furs away from me.

He had me flipped on to my stomach, and grabbed my hips to lift my lower body off the ground. I braced my knees apart, really spreading open for him. I was already swollen and soaked and so ready for that big, hard ribbed cock.

But he surprised me when he gripped my ass cheeks and spread them apart, running his wet nose over one cheek, along the small of my back, and then moving to the other cheek.

With my chest pressed to the ground, I tried to look over my shoulder, but he clamped his hand down on my nape and growled in want.

Wolf was the one in control.

What he didn't know, or maybe he did and that's why he acted so domineering and possessive, was that I liked this brutish alpha-hole-ness that came from him.

He gave my ass a hard swat, and I yelped, but then he dragged his tongue over the spot, easing the sting.

"Wolf—" his name was as far as I got before I felt his textured tongue slide along the crease and move along the puckered hole nestled between my cheeks. I felt my eyes widen, this wave of self-consciousness filling me.

He was... he was licking me back *there*. Oh, okay. This was how we would start the morning.

His claws dug into my ass, holding me open as he licked, as he teased that tiny opening that was like a direct line to my pussy because I got so wet for him.

"You're so fucking round and drenched." His voice was a serrated sound against my now soaked flesh before using the tip of his tongue to circle that opening. "And you're mine."

I popped my ass up further just as he pressed in, forcing that muscle inside of me, making me stretch and take what he had to give.

His snarling and growling only intensified the longer he ate out my ass, and the way he moved his tail to my ankle, it was clear he had to touch every part of me. That had my orgasm consuming me so suddenly I gave a startled yelp as it tore through my body.

With one more painful slap to my ass, Wolf rose, notched that bulbous, uncut cock at my entrance, and thrust into my pussy so forcefully I moved up on the ground, my head knocking into the rocky wall.

He gripped my waist and fucked me like the

beast he was, pulling me onto his cock as he thrust forward.

And when Wolf covered my back with his chest and latched those sharp teeth on the side of my neck, keeping me in place as he dominated me, I came again.

CHAPTER
SIXTEEN

Marcella

I was sore, but it was the good kind, the kind that gave you those little twinges that let you know you'd been loved *really* good and hard. Not that I knew what that actually felt like.

I hadn't been a virgin before Wolf, but I also had never been fucked like that either. In fact, I'd experienced nothing close to what I did with him.

And something had changed with him ever since we were finally together last night.

Although before we'd had sex—if something that primitive and savage could be called something so... mundane—I'd always catch him looking at me, being close to me.

But since last night? Wolf couldn't stop petting me.

He'd run his paw over the back of my head, his claws tangling in the strands, as he pulled me close and licked my face before dragging his tongue over my lips.

He made me sit on his lap as he fed me berries and nuts and salmon that he'd gathered just that morning.

Not that it was any hardship to let him do any of that. In fact, I just snuggled against him as he fed me and touched me, making me feel like there was nothing more important in the world than me.

I'd insisted he take me to the pond so I could clean up, which he'd responded with a lot of growling and snarling to let me know he didn't approve. But I wasn't about to walk around with dried cum between my legs and on my chest, because he liked the fact he marked me and I smelled like him.

The only way I talked him into it was by promising he could do it all over again tonight.

And something in my chest twinged at that thought. I didn't want to leave, not really, not right now, at least. I was curious to see how things could be with Wolf here.

Although realistically, it wasn't as if I could just completely drop off the face of the planet. There were people back home who would question where I was and what happened. I had to tie up loose ends.

Did I really, though? Who would miss me? Who would even care that I was gone?

Grandma is gone, and I don't have any friends. None that wanted anything to do with me unless they needed something.

Would Wolf even let me leave if I promised to come back? I glanced over at him as he packed a small satchel for me.

Even now he was thinking of my comfort, making sure we had a bladder of water and some food, so I didn't get hungry, because he informed me the trek to the cabin was quite a bit away.

I knew he wouldn't let me go, not willingly, not even if I swore up and down I would come back to him. In his eyes there was no him without me.

He helped me into my red peacoat and put the hood up, taking me out of my thoughts, his paws cupping each side of my head as he looked into my eyes.

"I want you to be warm," he murmured. "I can smell rain coming."

He stared into my eyes, made a deep sound in his

throat, and I rose on my toes so he could drag his tongue over my lips.

His version of a kiss that I was coming to love so much.

"Are you sure you want to travel today? The heavy storm will make it wet and cold, and the trip will be longer than normal."

I knew why he was bringing this up, that although he wanted to make me happy and would take me to the cabin, he was also worried. I didn't have to hear him say the words. Wolf was very expressive with the grunts and growls and entire body language that were displays of his emotions.

"I want to get my stuff, Wolf," I murmured, and reached up to run my finger along one thickly furred ear. He leaned into me as it twitched under my touch. "I won't run or try to escape, if that's what you think." I gave him a smile. "I enjoy being here with you." Not a lie, strangely enough.

How insane was it that in just a few days' time, I was so comfortable with him?

Not anymore. But of course I kept that to myself. If I admitted I had planned on getting away but then changed my mind, I was pretty sure he'd be too paranoid to even take the trip.

He made a gruff sound and leaned in to nuzzle my neck. I wrapped my arms around his waist, although my hands couldn't touch because he was just so big.

With one more lingering lick over my mouth that had my toes curling and a delicious hum of arousal filling me, he pulled back with an almost frustrated grunt and took my hand.

He grabbed the pack with the supplies in his other paw and we left the cave. Although it was sunny, rays of light peeking through the treetops that surrounded the cave, I glanced at Wolf.

"Are you sure it's supposed to storm?" I tipped my head back and looked at the bright blue sky. It was a gorgeous day, not too warm or cold.

He made that very animal-like sound when he found me amusing, and I cut a glare at him even though I knew he was just teasing.

"Trust me. I know when it's going to storm, my Little Bird."

And still we started our trek through the woods, keeping to the shadowy parts where the sunlight didn't quite reach.

I kept glancing at Wolf, and noticed how his ears would twitch from side to side as if he were picking up different sounds, and how he'd stop intermittently and tip his head back, his nostrils flaring as he inhaled deeply before we started walking again.

He was just so big and predator-esque, and here I was, this tiny human that didn't even reach the center of his chest, putting all my trust in him and knowing he'd never hurt me.

We stopped a few times, and he urged me to eat, growling low when I told him I wasn't hungry.

It was peaceful out here, with only the sound of the wind moving the leaves above us, birds chirping and squawking in the distance, and little critters scurrying about.

There was no car exhaust or honking horns. There were no screaming matches or the scent of cooking food from the street vendors.

It was just serene, and I closed my eyes as I rested my hands behind me to absorb it all.

I felt centered and grounded by it. I felt like... me.

When I opened my eyes and glanced at Wolf, feeling a smile tug at my lips, it was to see him already staring at me. "What?" I asked softly.

He shook his head. "Nothing and no one is prettier than you."

My belly flipped, my heart stopped, and before I

knew what I was doing, I was walking up to him and rising on my toes. I placed my hands on his chest and kissed the side of his mouth.

We continued our journey, Wolf insisting that we stop every so often so that I could rest, even though I told him we didn't have to. But I enjoyed taking our time.

I enjoyed being deep in the Alaskan woods, places few people had probably been because it was so wild and free. As time passed, the sky became darker and the promise of rain in the air became stronger.

Wolf stopped and glanced up, making a gruff sound, before looking at me. I suppressed rolling my eyes, knowing that the gleam in his eyes was his arrogance that he had been correct.

It was about to rain.

My thoughts clearly wanted to drive that stake home, because the skies opened up, and the rain fell down like a heavy blanket.

I laughed as it poured down my hands over my head in a poor excuse for an umbrella.

When I got to the outcropping, I turned and faced Wolf, seeing him standing right outside getting soaked, the water dripping off his dark fur, his teeth showing in that cute—and utterly endearing—wolfish smile of his.

"Get in here," I called out and laughed. He loped inside, and before I could brace myself, he did a full body, very canine shake.

Water droplets flung everywhere—including on me—but I was already soaked, so all I did was laugh harder.

I stood by the entrance to this little alcove and watched the rain fall. The sound of the droplets hitting leaves had this musical lithe to it. It was beautiful.

When I turned to face Wolf, I noticed he was perched on a boulder. Before I knew his intentions, he gripped my waist and adjusted me in his lap like I was some doll he could move around at his leisure.

He stared into my eyes for so long it made me feel bare. "What?" I asked softly.

"You fill this void in me I didn't know I had." He took my hand and placed it on his chest, right over his heart. "Right here. You fill me right here."

I softened against him and smiled. "Same," I whispered, not realizing how much I meant those words until they were out in the open.

Once Wolf had me positioned the way he

wanted, with our chests pressed against each other and my legs straddling his waist, he placed his enormous paw on the small of my back and leaned in to run his snout along the side of my throat.

"I've never smelled anything sweeter than you. You make my mouth water, my little human."

I let my head fall to the side and closed my eyes as he scented me. I couldn't explain the sensation I felt when he did this. It was a mixture of comfort and desire.

We just sat there, with Wolf smelling me as I ran my fingers through his thick fur. I could've fallen asleep this way, his colossal body cradling mine, the sound of the rain falling and birds calling out in the distance.

He was hard underneath my ass, that thick length digging into my flesh and causing me to squirm as my desire grew. I was a fiend for Wolf. His claws gripped me tighter, and he nosed my neck, pushing my hair away from my throat.

"Put me inside of you."

The way he said that, his tone serrated and dominating, as if I wouldn't dare deny him, had fresh moisture pooling in between my legs.

I didn't know how I got my pants off, but here

they were, my leggings hanging around one ankle, my pussy so wet I embarrassingly dripped my arousal onto his hard cock.

I looked between us, watching him grow harder, thicker, and couldn't stop myself from reaching down and stroking him from uncut tip to wide base.

I slid my fingers down to grip his heavy, fur covered balls, the weight substantial in my palm.

He gave a harsh groan and dragged his coarse tongue along the side of my neck before licking my cheek, then my mouth, and gently probing between my lips. He was also gentle, mindful of his sharp teeth. I sucked on his tongue, twirling mine along his much larger one, and lined the tip of his dick with my pussy hole. And then I slid down in one fluid motion.

Even though we had sex several times, I didn't think I'd ever be prepared or ready to take him. His size was just too monumental.

But I wanted that pain, wanted to feel the burning and stretching. I wanted Wolf to force his way inside, struggling because he was just so big and couldn't fully fit.

It was those thoughts and images in my mind, the feeling of his claws scraping up and down my back before he gripped my ass, that had me rising and falling back down.

I rode him hard and feverishly, not even sure who this woman was as I bounced on his dick and just let myself feel.

The smell of him, the sound of his groaning, and the feel of him inside of me, had me coming so hard and fast it shocked me so much I cried out.

He smacked my ass once, twice, and on the third time he gripped the flesh and pulled me down until our bodies were completely touching.

His cock jerked inside of me, and the feeling was so intense I felt another spark of ecstasy claim me. His cum was hot and thick inside of me, and I moaned, rotating my hips around, rolling them back-and-forth.

I wanted to stand up and have his seed slipping out of me and down my inner thighs. That nasty thought had me leaning in and sucking on his tongue again.

But just as my orgasm faded, he gripped my hips and lifted me off of him, his cock sliding out of me, all wet and sloppy from getting off on me.

When Wolf shoved me down to my knees, I lost my balance and rocked back. He gripped a chunk of my hair behind my head, tugging at the strands, and jerked me.

I moaned at how good that sting felt, how his focus was on my face, his eyes blazing with primal need.

Kneeling between his thighs brought me face-to-face with his cock, and I clenched my thighs and felt a flush steal over my breasts at how it jutted toward me.

He fisted his length, and I was riveted to the sight of how glossy his cock appeared, knowing all that wetness covered him because he was just buried deep inside my body.

Thick beads of cum dribbled out of the slit and before I could lean in and lick it clean, he ground out, "Suck me off and make me come again."

As I stared into his eyes, I gripped his shaft, my fingers not able to touch as I squeezed them around his erection.

I could feel the hard ribs that circled him, starting at the base and working their way up to stop right underneath the crown.

Tearing my focus away from Wolf's eyes, I looked down again and leaned forward, dragging my tongue over the bulbous head, sucking off that salty seed that spilled from him.

I hummed with pleasure and closed my eyes. I really started working him over, tracing those ribs, licking that definition like they were one of those rainbow suckers. He kept dribbling cum, and I kept licking it up.

Wolf spread his thighs a little further, allowing me to move in closer. He let go of his cock and leaned back, and when I couldn't reach with my mouth, I stroked with my palm. My eyes were closed as I lavished him, but they sprung open when I felt his paw on my ass, then between my cheeks.

He pressed the big pad of a digit against my asshole. He didn't penetrate me, couldn't with those sharp claws, but the digit was thick enough he could tease the hole and add pressure, which led to my pleasure growing.

I used my other hand to cup his sack, rolling the heavy twin weights in my palm. His balls overflowed in my palm, and the realization he was so virile and potent had me dripping wet.

My clit throbbed and my pussy clenched. The greedy bitch knew this cock needed to be between my thighs.

And then he started lifting his hips at the same time I sank my mouth down on him, forcing me to take more than comfortably possible.

I gagged, saliva spilling out from the corners of my mouth, my eyes watering.

Both paws were now in my hair, fisting the strands as he started fucking my mouth. I wasn't the one in control anymore. He was as he pounded into my face so savagely that all I could do was grip his thighs and hold on, letting him take his pleasure.

I squeezed my thighs together, pinching my clit between my pussy lips and humming at how good it felt. I could get off on this, just let my legs rub together and trap that tiny bundle of nerves as I moved my thighs back-and-forth until I got off.

And then he came, pushing my face all the way down until the crown was buried in the back of my throat and I had no choice but to swallow around it, drinking his cum that he pumped into my belly.

I couldn't breathe, was crying as my eyes watered profusely, but I was orgasming right along with him, explosions of pleasure starting in my pussy and spearing to the top of my head to the tips of my toes.

There was so much cum I couldn't swallow it fast enough, my mouth couldn't hold all of it. It sprayed out the sides, which elicited a huffing sound of pleasure from Wolf.

To feel his knot throbbing in my mouth, the ribs

hardening because he came, had me moaning again.

And when I swallowed the last spurt from him, he gently pulled my face away, cupped my cheeks, and leaned down to run his tongue over my face, licking at my tears, and smoothing that thick muscle along my lips so he was also tasting his seed.

"My perfect little mate. You're such a good girl." He gently ran those deadly claws over my cheeks. "No one will ever please me the way you do. No one will ever be as important to me as you are."

His praise did the most wonderful thing to me.

He continued to lick my lips, and I'd be lying if I didn't admit it turned me on, knowing that he didn't care about tasting his own seed as he kissed me.

In the next instance he had me on my back, my legs thrown over his shoulders, and his face buried in my pussy as he ate me out and got me off twice more.

It was long moments after both of us had orgasms that he just held me, keeping me draped over his chest as he laid on the hard ground.

He stroked his palm up and down my spine, petting me in that way that I loved so much.

And I twirled my fingers around his chest fur, closing my eyes and inhaling the scent of Wolf.

But when his body tensed, and his arms wrapped tightly around mine, I felt the air change. I felt the danger and aggression coming from Wolf so suddenly. My heart beat a strange rhythm. And that's when my survival instinct rose.

Something was wrong. Danger was in the air.

CHAPTER
SEVENTEEN

Marcella

Although I couldn't see the threat, I took Wolf's body language as a cue that something was very wrong.

Wolf had me off the ground and dressed in a matter of seconds, my clothes damp and sticking to my skin, but I didn't care. I was too on edge to worry about anything but whatever was causing Wolf to react like this.

And then he kept his colossal body in front of mine as he moved closer to the alcove entrance. I glanced around his bulging arm, but couldn't see anything.

With a hand placed on the center of his back, I

161

could feel how heavy he was breathing, his shoulders rising and falling because he was damn near panting.

I glanced down at his paws and watched as he clenched and relaxed them.

"Wolf?" I adjusted to the side, my tone frightened, but his arm shot out like a steel bar in front of me, stopping me from getting any closer.

I looked up at him, feeling my eyes widen, the fear almost consuming me. I could sense the violence and tension radiating off of him, and when he slowly turned his head to glance down at me, all I saw was the animal that he truly was reflected at me.

"I swear on the air in my lungs, the blood in my veins, and whatever good part of me I've ever had, that I won't let anything hurt you."

His words, the inclination of his voice, were so profound, so determined, that I knew it was his absolute truth.

What was out there that would make him say something with such conviction?

And then, as if whatever threat had heard my thoughts, a deep growl echoed through the woods.

With his big paw around my waist, he tightened his hold, pushing me further back into the alcove as he took a step forward and away from me.

"No matter what, you stay here. You let *me* protect *you*." He glanced at me once more. "It's what I was born to do."

My chest clenched at his words and I knew then —even if I hadn't already been certain—that I wouldn't leave Wolf. I was meant to be here.

We were meant to be together.

And I'd make that our reality if we got out of this... whatever *this* was.

I slowly nodded because I knew he wanted me to affirm I understood. Only then did Wolf face forward again. I saw the way his shoulders rose and fell as he breathed harder.

His paws were completely outstretched on either side of him now, his claws seeming darker and sharper than ever before.

I leaned to the side to look around his bicep for a prolonged moment.

No sound escaped me as I watched the creature step out from the thickness of the forest. I could tell it was another beast-creature like Wolf, but aside from the height and overall shape, that's where the similarities ended.

This creature looked rabid and emaciated. It had

white and red foam—the latter color I had to assume was blood—spilling out of the corners of his jaw, and around its discolored teeth. One of its ears was partially missing, and I could see chunks of fur gone, scars covering its flesh underneath.

On instinct, I moved back another step just as Wolf took one forward, keeping his body in front of mine.

The sounds coming from him were ones I'd never heard before. His growls were much harsher, and I knew they were ones of warning.

My heart was thundering, and I knew there was nothing I could do. As strong as I thought I was, as independent as I'd always been in my life, this was something I never even conceived of going up against.

And then, like a crack of lightning and a boom of thunder, the two beasts crashed together.

For as malnourished and sickly as the other animal appeared, he fought just as brutally as Wolf. But what made the entire situation even more terrifying was the way the other beast kept looking at me with his jaw opened wide and his eyes flashing with hunger.

What kind of hunger it was, I didn't want to find out.

He tried to get to me repeatedly, but before he could get close enough, Wolf locked his jaws and claws into its body and hauled it back.

There was a deafening roar from Wolf before he gripped the other creature and threw him against the nearest tree. Its body cracked against the trunk, the sound coming from it so unnatural it had bile rising in my throat.

It fell to the ground and stayed there unmoving. Optimistically, I hoped this was the end, that in its weakened state it was no match for my Wolf.

When it stayed on the ground, I tentatively moved forward. Wolf stood a few feet from the creature's body, his chest rising and falling, blood dripping off of his claws from when he tore into the animal.

Slowly, I started making my way toward Wolf, my gaze never leaving the other animal. And then Wolf turned slowly toward me.

"My female," he said, low and deep and full of relief.

I was about to go running into his arms, needing to hold him and reassure myself we were both safe, but in the next second the other beast hissed out and was off the ground, hauling himself toward Wolf.

Both creatures crashed together, and I screamed as I stumbled back, losing my footing before falling to the forest ground.

It clawed at Wolf, tearing at his chest until I saw dark stains from blood mat his fur. I screamed, but the sound fell on deaf ears and was pointless.

I couldn't just stand here and let this happen, so I stood and found the largest rock I could pick up.

Without thinking about my safety or how stupid I was currently being going after something that could split me in half, I launched myself at the other creature and brought the rock down on its skull.

It roared out and swiped out, its claws barely missing my flesh as it rendered the material of my shirt that covered my abdomen.

It didn't stop me from bringing that stone down again and again, right over its boxy skull, until I smelled the metallic tang of blood coating the air.

With one more hard slam of the stone against its skull, the creature fell to the side, the gaping wound on the back of its head so vividly disgusting, I nearly gagged.

The forest ground became saturated with its blood, its lifeless eyes fixated above, unblinking.

I dropped the stone and stumbled back, unable

to catch my breath as I stared at Wolf, who was watching me with this eerily calm expression.

He had four long gouges down the front of his chest, but he didn't seem like it bothered him as he slowly rose, his colossal form towering over mine. His head lowered and his gaze locked on me.

"My fierce female," he rumbled out, and I shivered, taking a step back, although I wasn't sure why.

I wasn't afraid, not of Wolf. Never of him. There was just something in the way he looked at me, in the tone of his voice, that had my blood pumping for a very different reason.

My skin felt tight, tingly, and I took another step back, and one more. He made an indistinct sound deep within his chest and I felt this flash of heat and a rush of adrenaline soar through every part of me.

He stalked forward, his dick growing erect. My mouth dried and my heart raced. And before I knew what was happening, Wolf reached out and grabbed my throat, yanking me forward so he could drag his nose up and down the side of my throat, scenting me.

He pulled back enough to breathe harshly against the shell of my ear, then warned, "run."

CHAPTER

EIGHTEEN

Wolf

I felt the thrill of the hunt rush through me as I chased my Marcella through the woods. Blood covered me, and adrenaline pumped through my veins because of the fight with the rogue creature.

The crazy bastard was starved and wanted my mate. But before I could kill him, my perfect female had taken matters into her own hands and done the job with so much fierceness I felt a swell of pride fill me.

And because of that fight, I was feral, primal, and all I wanted to do was tackle Marcella to the ground, tear away her clothing and rut between her thighs.

I needed to because she was mine and this was the only way I could ensure that, to show her exactly the male she was now tied to for the rest of our lives.

Because I wouldn't let her go. Never.

"My Little Bird is fast." My voice was low, but it carried in the wind as I taunted her. Reaching her would have been effortless, but the hunt, the chase, had my cock hard, the length bobbing as I ran faster.

I could hear her heart racing, and smelled how wet she was.

"Is your pussy ready for me, my fragile human?"

She sucked in a sharp breath, but didn't answer.

"Are you aching for me to fill you up like I have so much these past few days?"

I paced myself, because I knew as soon as I caught her it would be over. I'd be fierce in my claiming of her, far harder than any other time.

The only way for me to get out all this aggression, possessiveness, and alpha need in me was to fuck my Marcella so hard anything and anyone close enough to hear or see us would know she was mine.

I let her think she was faster because it turned me on even more. I smelled the slight hint of her fear. She might know I'd never hurt her, but she also sensed how wild I was right now. She knew I was treading a thin line of civility, of sanity.

I dropped to all fours and weaved between the trees as I ate up the distance.

My Little Bird was quick.

No more playing. No more chasing. I wrapped a forearm around her middle and hauled her off the ground. She cried out in surprise, and I growled in pleasure at the sound.

She pressed against the trunk of the tree after I turned us.

I wasn't conscious of anything but fucking her as I tore away her clothes until they were tatters of material around us. I snarled and gripped her waist as I pulled her ass out so her upper body was parallel with the ground, her pussy ripe for the taking.

I couldn't have spoken even if I wanted to, and so I used my foot to kick her legs apart, and my good girl knew exactly what I wanted.

She spread for me so nicely, so quickly. Her pussy lips opened like flower petals, and any kind of humanity faded as I let my feral side take full control.

"Pink, perfect, wet cunt," I hissed as I crouched,

placed my paws on her ass cheeks, and spread her even wider.

I went feral on her sloppy pussy, licking, sucking, feeling her tremble for me. And when I shoved my tongue into her, making her take the thick muscle with no warning, she was my good girl and gave me her orgasm.

Her pussy gripped my tongue, squeezing the muscles. I felt my cock drip cum onto the forest floor, throb and jerk with the need to be tried in her tight body.

"Tell your mate you want me to fuck you." My voice was barely recognizable as my animal side took control.

"Wolf," she moaned, and shook her ass, the mounds jiggling.

I smacked her ass once, twice, and a third time before dragging my tongue over her slit once more, drinking her honey, and stood.

Taking hold of my length, I lifted it, smacking her cunt with the thick head. The wet sound of flesh against flesh pulled a groan from me.

"You feel how hard you make me, little thing?"

She moaned.

"You want an animal fucking you between these sweet thighs?"

"Wolf. God—"

"I don't want your God's name on your tongue, Marcella. You should scream my name instead." I lodged the head in her pussy hole, dug my claws into her hips, and shoved in deep and rough. "Bare your neck."

She pushed her hair off her shoulder and tipped her head to the side, letting me see that slender, creamy length. My mouth watered, saliva slipping off my sharp teeth.

"I've never been hungrier." I fucked her with a frenzy that consumed me. I'd bruise her, mark my Little Bird so she'd be sore and wouldn't be able to walk straight tomorrow. She wouldn't be able to sit comfortably.

A hum left me, and I forced myself into her when she cried out, when she told me to slow down.

"I can't and won't."

She gasped and cried out when I pulled out and slammed back in. "Right there. Don't stop."

Never.

I let my tail slip up the side of her thigh, over her hip, and started tickling her clit as I pushed in and pulled out like a savage. With my other paw I reached around and grabbed her fat tit, tweaking the nipple between the pads of my fingers, pulling it hard enough I knew it hurt.

"You'll be so full of my seed that there won't be any way I don't get you full of my pups." Her cunt juices made my thrusting fluid as it coated her inner thighs and covered my shaft. "I need you big and pregnant with my young." My cock jerked at the thought and I spurted cum into her.

"I—I can feel you, Wolf."

I purred and came into her a little more. "There's more where that came from, sweet thing. There's more seed I have to give you. My balls are full of cum just for you." I tipped my head back and howled as the pleasure became too much. "There won't ever be anyone or anything that makes me feel as good as you do. There won't be anyone who pleases me as much as you do, my Marcella."

"Oh... Wolf. Here I—"

"—come for me." I bent over her back and sank my teeth into her throat and we both came. I saw stars, my nuts pulling up, my knot fully swollen and locked inside of her, so I couldn't move.

"That's it. Take it all." The muffled words vibrated against her throat. I pulled back enough to lick at her blood. When I rose, my cock still pulsed in her pussy, my cum still shooting out of me. I

173

exhaled, my entire body shaking from the force of how good she felt.

She sagged against the tree, her blunt little nails dug into the bark, her breathing harsh and loud all around us.

Finally, my cock pulsed one last time before I stilled and exhaled. We didn't move or speak for long seconds as I let my knot do its thing and stayed locked in her so my cum couldn't escape, so I could get her pregnant with my baby.

"Say it," I demanded and dragged my tongue up the length of her spine, licking the blood that welled from the scratches I wasn't even aware I'd given her, drinking the salty sweat that covered her skin. "Be my good girl and tell me what I want to hear, and I'll get you off twice more, Little Bird."

She was still breathing hard, but turned her head to the side, stared me in the eyes, and whispered, "You know I'm yours. And nothing will ever change that."

CHAPTER
NINETEEN

Wolf

I stayed within the shadows as I watched Marcella speak with the old human.

I trusted my little human, knew that she wouldn't leave, but the urge to go to her, to place my body between hers and anything and anyone that could take her from me, rode me strong.

But I forced myself to stay back, reaching out and gripping the thick trunk of a cedar tree, my claws digging into the bark until I left deep gouges.

I waited and listened as she told him there was a change of plans, that she made other arrangements and would stay here longer.

Once we reached her cabin two days before, I hadn't been in a hurry to make the trek back to my lair. I wanted her to rest. I needed her to eat and drink. I knew she was sore from everything that had happened, and all I wanted to do was take care of her.

So I stood guard as she sat by the shore and drew. I watched her make shapes using colors from these thin sticks she held. Pencils, she called them.

She made beautiful pictures of our surroundings, and I wanted to take them back and press them to the cavern walls of our lair, coloring the dark space with her light.

And at night I held her, letting her use my body for cushioning and warmth as I wrapped my arms around her, my tail curled around her waist.

When she was sound asleep, I prowled outside, stalking the familiar trails and land surrounding the cabin.

But now here we were, the day she told me she was supposed to leave, a boat coming to pick her up. I became surly at the thought of anyone getting close to her. I became territorial at the thought of anyone even looking at her.

But if I wanted her to trust me, I had to do the same.

And so I stood back and watched, stayed hidden and let my perfect female control the situation. *Just this once.*

Even from a distance I could smell his apprehension, saw the way his wrinkled face took on an inquisitive, maybe even slightly concerned expression.

He wasn't a fool. Age and experience had made him wary. He might've even heard about my kind over the years, fables about the beastly wolves that lived deep within the Alaskan wilderness.

But he finally gave a nod and turned to leave. My Marcella stood by the shore, watching until he rounded the bend and was out of sight.

When she turned, I expected to see a little apprehension, maybe even regret, on her face that she made the wrong decision. But what she gave me was the prettiest smile I'd ever seen.

She took a step toward me and I moved out from the shadows of the forest. And then she ran to me. I held my arms out just as Marcella jumped into them, wrapping her legs around my waist, her arms around my neck.

I buried my snout in her hair, inhaling deeply and letting out a very pleased rumble.

"My Marcella," I said softly, and slid one paw

down to cup her ass, the glorious mounds overfilling my palm. "Mine."

EPILOGUE

Marcella

I was sore, sweaty, and cum was a steady flow out of my pussy, making me drenched between my thighs and getting the furs beneath me all sticky.

"Have I told you I love the way you smell after I fuck you good and hard?"

I laughed softly, but I was so tired, my body fantastically spent that it didn't sound as energetic as it normally would have.

"It's because you insist on coming so much, then smearing it into my body like it's lotion."

He grunted, clearly pleased with that description.

JENIKA SNOW

I looked over at Wolf as he made his way down my belly, over my hip, and dragged his tongue along my thigh and calf.

He circled my ankle with his fingers and lifted my leg, drawing his tongue over the arch before licking my toes and the top of my foot.

I'd never been more sated or happy in my life, especially as I felt Wolf start his nightly routine of licking every single inch of me after he fucked me raw.

This part of aftercare he provided me brought our entire sexual encounter full circle. And it was because he truly enjoyed doing this. It was one extra layer to Wolf that I was finding I loved about him more each day.

Over the last several months, I got used to this very different lifestyle. Although everything had been so easily accessible in the city, as the time passed and I got accustomed to living in the wild, I realized none of that materialistic stuff mattered. None of it had made me happy.

Wolf filled a void inside of me I hadn't realized I had. He taught me how to hunt and fish, how to pick berries and mushrooms that were safe for us to eat.

He showed me how to skin an animal, which was my least favorite thing. I was too much of an

180

animal lover, even if it was necessary for our survival.

He gave me one last lick before settling down beside me, his forearm flung over my body, his paw molding against my belly.

I placed my much smaller hand over his, smiling. It wasn't just about us anymore. We had a little one on the way.

Wolf held me as I thought about the things I'd initially missed. Cheeseburgers from Rowdy's, the local fast food place in the city. Or enjoying hot fudge sundaes while binging mindless reality TV and drinking a bottle of wine on a Saturday night.

But even after missing those things, they didn't compare to how perfect this new life was with Wolf.

My stomach gave a sudden growl, and I felt my cheeks heat as I chuckled when I heard Wolf do that familiar grunt of amusement.

"Is my little one growing big and strong inside my tiny human, telling us he's hungry?"

"He?" I looked over my shoulder. "Could be a girl." I turned to face him fully and pressed my cheek against his furry chest, just inhaling the wild scent of him.

"Girl. Boy. Makes no difference. Eventually, we'll have a slew of them."

I snorted. "Wishful thinking, buddy." But secretly, that sounded like heaven.

I inhaled again. He always had the smell of night air clinging to him. With the temperatures dropping as fall approached, we were keeping more inside. But that sure as hell wasn't a hardship. It allowed me to snuggle against him even more and let his warmth act like a natural heater.

He kept his palm on my belly, stroking the rounded mound. I was just about to doze off when I felt a fluttering in my abdomen. His expression told me he hadn't felt it.

When I glanced down the length of my body, I held my breath as I watched his paw move slow circles around my bump. And then I felt it again, this time harder.

A soft sound of surprise left me, and Wolf jerked back. I started laughing at the strange look on his face. He shifted back slightly so he could really look at my stomach.

"Did you feel it?" Although he didn't have to answer for me to know that he did. His body language spoke volumes.

I reached out and gripped his wrist, bringing his paw back to my belly. His palm was just so large that it nearly encompassed the entire width. And as we both lay there in silence, waiting for it to happen again, I felt that love I had for Wolf growing even more.

I didn't know when it happened, but it had definitely snuck up on me. It was this feeling that was now so embedded in me it would only grow. With time, it would get bigger and stronger. It would become impenetrable.

"Mine," he rumbled out, and moved down the fur so that he could drag his tongue over my baby bump.

There was another nudge and then he was resting his cheek against me, murmuring soft words that I couldn't hear, ones I knew were just for our little one.

As I lay on our pallet and ran my fingers over his head and around his ears, I knew there was no better happily ever after that I could get than with my big bad wolf.

The End.

ABOUT THE AUTHOR

Want a **FREE** read? Grab your copy here:
https://dl.bookfunnel.com/70kysmttbw

Find Jenika at:

www.JenikaSnow.com
Jenika_Snow@yahoo.com

Manufactured by Amazon.ca
Bolton, ON

34248310R00105